MOBY
DICK

Retold by Janet Nicola Tufts

Contents

CHAPTER 1

An Explanation

You may wonder what kind of person would choose to spend three or four years of his precious life on a ship at sea. You may wonder even further who would go out to sea on, of all ships, a whaling ship. Let me introduce myself. My name is Ishmael, and I am a person who has gone to sea on a three-year whaling voyage in pursuit of the largest creature in the world, the whale.

It was many years ago, some time in the early 1800s, when I found myself rather bored with the things being offered to me on land. I decided it was time once again for me to venture out to sea. You must understand that for people like me the sea has a way of nourishing the soul. Such pure air does wonderful things to the lungs.

You may ask, why not go to sea as a passenger? Surely that would mend the spirit better than anything. Agreeably, yes, but it so happened that at this particular time in my life I was without much money. To be a passenger one needs money. Please don't feel sorry for me because, even if I had money, I would not want to be a passenger. Passengers get seasick and grumpy and are not a lot of fun to be with.

Your next question: How about going to sea as a commodore, or a captain, or a cook? No, no, no, it is enough for me to look after myself let alone look after a ship.

When I went to sea, I went as a sailor. I was ordered about, but one gets used to that. Who in this world doesn't get ordered about, if not by someone, well then, by something? When the sea captain shouted at me to sweep the deck, I didn't mind because at least I was being paid for my trouble. And what is more marvellous in this world than being paid for something? Yes, I'd certainly rather be a paid sailor than a paying passenger!

Now that I've shown why the life of a sailor was perfect for me, I still must somehow explain how I ended up, on this particular occasion, as a sailor of a whaling ship (up to this point, I had always been a merchant sailor). Here I draw a blank. Somewhere, somehow, a decision was made for me which I could not seem to change. Something told me that being a sailor on a whaling voyage was part of my destiny. I have no other reasonable explanation except perhaps to say that I had an interest in the great whale. The dangerous tales that had been told of such a mysterious monster living in the wild and distant seas aroused my curiosity. So, if an explanation is needed, that, I suppose, is it.

I stuffed a shirt or two in my old bag, headed for the New England Coast, and so began my own dangerous tale of the great whale.

CHAPTER 2

A Decent Harpooner

It was a Saturday night in December when I arrived at a place called New Bedford and was disappointed to learn that I had missed the boat to the original and most famous American whaling port, Nantucket Island. Even though New Bedford's whaling business had grown larger than Nantucket's, I had made up my mind to depart on my whaling voyage from Nantucket.

The next boat to Nantucket wasn't leaving for two days so my first task was to find a place to eat and sleep. You may recall I had very little money, which meant I was not in a position to be choosy. There I was, on a dark and dreary night, and knowing no one, pacing the streets to find the least expensive inn in New Bedford.

The "Crossed Harpoons" and "The Sword-Fish Inn" looked too classy. Then I came to "The Spouter Inn:—innkeeper Peter Coffin." It looked more reasonable, but it was eerie that the sign above the door connected the whale (with its spout) to a coffin. Would I end up in a coffin if I went whaling? Should I go in? Looking around and not seeing many other choices, I entered the inn.

On one wall hung a very large oil painting, but because of the smokiness and poor lighting in the room, I couldn't see much more than patches of colors and shadows. Something made me stare longer at the painting. In the middle of all the wild blues was a big black mass covering three painted lines. I suddenly realized what I was looking at: an exhausted whale in the midst of a great hurricane crashing down on a ship and breaking its three masts. People were being frantically tossed everywhere. The whale. A coffin. I was getting spooked.

Clubs and spears covered the opposite wall and I shuddered at the thought of the savages that once held those tools. Bent and rusty whaling harpoons and lances were mixed in with the other items. One story told of the lance on the farthest right being used by a man who killed fifteen whales in one day.

I hunted down the landlord, Mr. Coffin, and requested a room for the night. After answering that his house was full, he paused for a second and added, "Do you have a problem with sharing a room with a harpooner?"

I was unsure, but not having much choice, I told Mr. Coffin that if the harpooner was a decent fellow I'd agree to sharing a bed for a night or two.

"I thought so," said the landlord. "You look friendly. You'd have to be if you're going whaling. Can't go whaling if you aren't able to get

along with others. And now, how about some supper?"

During a filling meal of meat and potatoes and dumplings, I asked a few questions about my harpooner who had not yet appeared. When the landlord told me that he never ate dumplings, only steak, and that he liked his steaks so rare that they were almost raw, I began to worry. What kind of a beast had I agreed to sleep with?

The more I wondered about this harpooner, the more I disliked the idea of sleeping with him. I was certain his clothes would be dirty and fishy smelling. I began to shiver all over. It was getting late and I knew that any decent harpooner would be home and heading to bed by now. What would I do if he stumbled into bed during the black of the night? How would I know from what filthy place he had come?

"Mr. Coffin! I've changed my mind about sleeping with that harpooner. I think I'll try this bench here."

Mr. Coffin was good enough to dust off the bench, and I took a good, long look. It was, without a doubt, much shorter than me and much skinnier. Nevertheless, I was determined to make it work. After trying all kinds of positions, I finally gave up and decided that perhaps I had been too hard on this unknown harpooner. I'd wait awhile and when he arrived I'd greet him with a handshake and introduce myself. Who knows, perhaps we would become jolly good friends.

Throughout the evening the other boarders came strolling in bit by bit but still I saw no sign of my harpooner. Growing impatient, I demanded that Mr. Coffin tell me who and what this harpooner was, and whether or not I would be safe spending the night with him.

"He pays regularly so he's certainly not all bad," the landlord replied. "But I suppose you won't see him tonight after all. As for you, it is getting late and you'd be best to forget about him and get some sleep."

Agreeing, I climbed the stairs and entered the small cold room. I couldn't help staring at the big bed with uneasiness. As my eyes stretched to the corner of the room, I noticed a seaman's bag belonging to the harpooner in a heap on the floor. Above, on a hook, was an item of clothing that looked no better than a matted carpet. Surely this harpooner did not walk the streets in public wearing a carpet! Slowly I undressed myself, pausing and thinking as I removed each item of clothing *I can leave now, before it's too late*. Suddenly, I found that I was half undressed and too cold to do anything else but hop into bed.

I tossed and turned for a long time on that rocky mattress which was no better than that too-small bench, but at last I dozed off into a light sleep. Later, in the black of the night as I had feared, I heard footsteps in the passageway.

This must be the harpooner. Please help me. I demanded my body to lie perfectly still

15

and swore myself to silence. After entering the room, the harpooner lit a small lantern and went straight to his seaman's bag. He began working at the knots to unlace it. I strained, without success, to get a look at his face. All of a sudden, with his bag finally untied, he turned around—good heavens! What a sight! What a face! It was dark and purplish with large blackish squares plastered all over it. I was right, he was a terrible bedmate! I wasn't safe at all. He'd been in a fight and had gone to a doctor to have himself bandaged up. But wait—when he moved into the light I saw that I was mistaken. Those were not bandages on his face after all, but tattoos. I regained control and scolded myself for judging this man completely by his skin. After all, a man can be honest no matter what color he is.

As all these incredible thoughts were going through my mind, the harpooner appeared not to notice me at all. He removed his hat and I saw he had no hair except for a small scalp-

knot twisted up on his purplish forehead. Immediately, my eyes darted back and forth from his head to his tomahawk on the bedside table. Now, I am not a coward, but I desperately wanted to bolt out that door. I feared, however, that if I even moved an inch, I'd be scalped in an instant. I was frozen in terror.

As the harpooner began undressing, I tell you with no amount of exaggeration that purple tattoos covered every inch of his body. He must have been some savage from the ends of the earth! And here he was, ready for bed, jumping right in beside me!

"Landlord! Help! Mr. Coffin, please save me!" was all I could yell.

Grabbing his tomahawk, the savage growled, "Who are you? Where did you come from? Speak! Tell me or I'll kill you!"

At that precise moment the landlord entered and I ran to him for safety. To my surprise, he chuckled and said, "Relax. Queequeg wouldn't hurt a hair on your head."

"Stop grinning," I said. "Why didn't you tell me he was so savage-looking?"

Looking a little hurt, Queequeg motioned for me to climb back into bed and very kindly straightened out the sheets. I stared at him for a moment. Despite all his tattoos, he looked clean and almost gentle. What a fuss I'd been making; he had every right to be as afraid of me as I was of him.

"Good night," I said to the landlord, "and I'm sorry for disturbing you." And without any more fuss, I climbed into bed and had the best sleep of my life.

I awoke about daylight the next morning to find Queequeg's tattooed arm thrown over me in a most protective and caring way. I was no longer afraid, but this hugging (I guess you would call it that) certainly gave me a strange feeling. I wasn't sure if I should feel touched, or if I should feel bothered, or whether it was best just to laugh. I decided to wake him by yelling "Queequeg!" in his ear. He only continued to snore, but I didn't quit.

"Queequeg! For goodness sakes, Queequeg, wake up! Wake up now!"

He let out a grunt and quickly withdrew his arm. His body shook like a big shaggy dog just getting out of the water. He sat up in bed and rubbed his eyes as if trying hard to remember how it happened that I was in that room with him. At last he stood up and told

me that he would dress first and leave the room so that I'd be able to dress in private. How very considerate of him! Thinking how rude I had been the previous night, I was filled with guilt.

Queequeg first removed every bit of his clothing. He then put on his beaver hat and, with nothing else but his hat on, grabbed his boots and climbed under the bed. Why he needed privacy for putting his boots on I'll never know, but the gruntings and groanings that came from under the bed were astounding. At last he appeared, with his hat squashed and bent over his eyes, and limped around the room with his toes obviously pinched in his boots.

Aware that there was a window in the center of the room and that anyone on the main street could easily see in, I asked Queequeg to quickly put on his pants. He did and then began an energetic cleaning at the washstand. What I saw next you will not believe. With a lathered face ready for shaving, he reached for his harpoon from the bed corner and, after sharpening its head on his boot, he began shaving (or shall I say 'harpooning') his face. When later I learned of what fine steel a harpoon is made and how very sharp it is, I admired Queequeg's clever use of it.

Finishing the rest of his routine, Queequeg grabbed his harpoon and proudly marched out of the room. From there, we went our separate ways. At the end of the day when I returned to the Spouter-Inn, I found Queequeg sitting before the fire with a large book on his lap. He was busy counting the pages of the book. What interested me was that when he got to fifty, he paused, looked around, and whistled in amazement. Then he would begin counting again from number one, stopping again and again at every fiftieth page. I suppose that he could only count to fifty. No matter, he was obviously getting a great amount of enjoyment in the number of groups of fifty in this large book.

As savage looking as he was with his marked face, you could not hide this man's soul. Here he was getting excited about something so utterly simple. This was a man with an honest heart.

As I studied Queequeg, he never so much as glanced at me. I found this rather odd considering that we had not only shared the same bed the night before, but had woken up in a rather friendly position. But that was Queequeg's way, quiet and content to be by himself. All of a sudden, my heart melted and I sat down beside him. We looked over the book together and I tried to explain to him the meaning of the printed words. Before long, we were involved in a heavy discussion and from then on, we were lifelong friends. He said he would gladly die for me.

CHAPTER 3

A Queer Old Boat

The next day was Monday and our day of departure for Nantucket. Queequeg and I borrowed a wheelbarrow to haul our belongings down to the wharf. As we said good-bye to the landlord, he had a good chuckle over the fact that Queequeg and I had become such devoted companions, especially after my frenzied state the first night.

As we walked along shifting the wheelbarrow from my hand to his, Queequeg told me a funny story about the first wheelbarrow he had ever seen. It had been lent to him by an old seaman who thought his bag looked too heavy to carry up the road to the inn. Trying not to look like he didn't know what to do with it—even though he truly didn't—Quee-queg tied his bag to the wheelbarrow and tossed the whole thing over his head onto his shoulders and marched away. I could picture Queequeg, only wanting to be polite, carrying the wheelbarrow and it made me laugh.

At last, with our luggage on board the schooner and our passage paid, the sails were hoisted and we set off for Nantucket. Heading into open water and picking up speed, Quee-queg and I both drank in the fresh air as if without it a minute longer we might die. So absorbed were we that we almost didn't notice the simpleton standing behind us mak-ing fun of Queequeg's appearance. Oh dear! I was sure that this would be the end of the bumpkin. Queequeg turned, grabbed the fel-low, and tossed him with such strength that he somersaulted backwards high in the air and somehow miraculously landed on his feet at the stern of the boat. Queequeg acted as if he had tossed an old shoe in a garbage pail.

"Captain! Captain!" cried the simpleton. "Who does that beast think he is?"

"Hello, sir," demanded the captain, "what do you think you're doing? You could have killed that fellow."

"Kill?" said Queequeg. "I'll not kill him. He's too small. I'm off to kill a big whale."

"I'll kill you," roared the captain, "if you try anything like that again!"

Now it just so happened that the captain should have been watching what he was doing. He had let the boom, the long heavy pole that holds the bottom of the mainsail, fly from side to side. The flying boom knocked the poor fellow who Queequeg had manhandled in the head and tossed him into the wild sea. Panic broke. No one knew what to do except Queequeg, who immediately crawled under the boom, grabbed a rope and secured the boom in its proper place. Without hesitation, he then stripped to the waist and dove in after the drowning victim. What a strong and splendid man he was, swimming madly in search of a body that was nowhere in sight. Queequeg took one last look and then dove down under water. A few minutes later, he rose again dragging the coughing and sputtering victim. Queequeg was voted a hero and the captain apologized for his earlier behavior.

The remainder of our trip was quite uneventful compared to the rescue of the simpleton and we safely arrived on the island of Nantucket. Have you ever been to Nantucket? On a map it looks so lonely standing on its own away from the shore. It's hard to imagine it as a real place with real people and a real history. Listen to the wondrous story that tells how the red-men settled the island: as the legend goes, in olden times an eagle descended upon the New England coast of America and snatched up a baby Indian in its talons. The parents of the child cried in desperation as they saw their child carried out of sight. They

decided to follow the path of the eagle across the wide waters, and thus discovered the island. To their grief, however, they found the little Indian's skeleton in an ivory coffin.

Born on the beach, the Nantucketers naturally made a living off the sea. In the beginning, they started by digging for crabs in the sand and then, gaining courage, began wading out with nets for mackerel. Becoming more experienced, they began to take their boats out for cod until they were confident enough to send great fleets of ships out to capture whales. And so, the Nantucketers conquered the watery world!

It was late in the evening when Queequeg and I went ashore in search of the hotel the "Try Pots" recommended to us by Mr. Coffin. It was famous for its seafood chowders, and after spending a few days there, I most certainly could see why! We ate chowder for breakfast, lunch, and dinner until we could almost see scales replacing our skin. One meal I was sure I saw a live eel in my chowder and asked Queequeg to go fetch his harpoon.

While discussing our plans for the next day, I was surprised to learn that Queequeg had already decided that I was to select our sailing vessel. I knew nothing about whaling ships and told Queequeg I was quite unimpressed with his plan. I was counting on his advice in this important decision. It was no use; Queequeg insisted I go. He said he had great confidence in me, but I really think he was looking forward to some extra hours in bed! In the morning, without arguing any further, I set out to inquire about available ships.

After investigating three boats I selected the perfect one for us—the *Pequod*. It was a queer old boat, not magnificent in any way, but with a weathered look that seemed to say, "I've seen it all!" In my search for someone in charge, I ran into a man who was as weathered looking as the boat.

"Are you the captain of the *Pequod*?" I asked the wrinkly old man.

"And what if I were?" he responded, "What do you want?"

"I was thinking of going whaling," I said hopefully.

"I see you are no Nantucketer. Do you know anything about whaling?" he questioned.

"Nothing, sir. But I have been on four merchant ships."

"Don't talk to me about merchant ships!" he roared. "They don't count for anything! Now tell me, why would a nice fellow like you want to try whaling?"

"I want to see what it is, sir. I want to see some excitement and danger," I said.

"You want to see danger, eh? Well, have you seen Captain Ahab?"

"Who is Captain Ahab?"

"Captain Ahab! Why he's the captain of this ship," he laughed.

"I thought you were the captain," I said.

"Oh, I am a captain all right—a retired one. Captain Peleg's the name. I own this boat along with Captain Bildad. It is up to us to make sure that this ship is prepared for a voyage. We gather all her supplies and choose her crew. Now if you really want to learn about the dangers of whaling, I can send you in the direction of Captain Ahab. You'll find, young man, that he only has one leg."

"Was it a whaling accident?" I trembled a little.

"Come closer," he whispered. "His leg was swallowed in one single gulp by the biggest monstrosity of a whale that you could imagine!" I tried to be calm. "Now," he continued, "are you having second thoughts about going whaling? Are you the type of man who can pitch a harpoon into a whale's back and then go after it? Are you?"

"Yes, sir," I stammered, "I, I am."

"Good. Now you said you want to see excitement. Go to the bow of the boat and peer overboard," he demanded. I did as I was told. "Tell me, young man, what do you see?"

"Why nothing but water, sir," I answered.

"Well, what do you think about seeing excitement?" he said sounding very smart. "For most days in three long years that's all you'll see. Water."

I would not be discouraged by this old whaleman. I had decided to go a-whaling and a-whaling I would go. Seeing my determination, Captain Peleg lead me below the deck to sign the papers and meet Captain Bildad.

Captain Bildad, like Captain Peleg, was a retired whaleman who was making loads of money lending out his ships and collecting the profits of the whale killings. He was a tough businessman. He also had a poor reputation from his seagoing days. It was told in Nantucket that when his ship returned home, the crew collapsed from exhaustion, one by one, as they stepped onto shore. He had a hard heart, and it was he who sat across from me at this very moment. Peleg introduced me, "Bildad, this man says he wants our ship. What do you think of him?"

"He'll do," was all Bildad said and he proceeded to gather pen and ink for signing.

As I said, this man was a hard businessman and money was the topic of discussion at this point. In whaling, you are not paid a salary, but you earn a certain amount of the money made from the whales killed on the voyage. This amount is called a "lay." The higher your position on board or the more experience you have, the higher your lay will be. Well, the nerve of Bildad! The lay he gave me was nothing but an insult. After much arguing, we finally came up with an acceptable amount. I asked then if I could meet Captain Ahab, and both Peleg and Bildad agreed that it would not be a good idea. I was puzzled but put Ahab out of my mind for the present time.

Feeling as though I had accomplished a good day's work, I headed back to the "Try Pots" to tell my news to Queequeg. He seemed most satisfied and the next day, after our breakfast of chowder, we walked down to the *Pequod*. Queequeg was interested in what lay the captains might give him.

Almost immediately, we spotted Captain Peleg who, having a good look at Queequeg's harpoon, remarked, "Good quality. Looks like you know harpoons. And you handle it just right. I say, Quohog, or whatever your name is, have you ever killed a whale?"

In an instant Queequeg was on the upper deck taking aim with his harpoon. "Captain, you see that small bit of wood floating over there on the water behind Captain Bildad's head? Suppose that was a whale's eye." Suddenly, he shot his harpoon, brushing Bildad's hat as it flew past. The harpoon struck that wood right out of sight! "Why," Queequeg said proudly, "that whale's dead!"

"Quick, Peleg," said Bildad, "run and get the ship's papers. Hedgehog, I mean Quohog, we must have you on our boat. Come and sign."

And with that, Queequeg received the largest lay that was ever given to a harpooner out of Nantucket.

CHAPTER 4

Our Mysterious Captain

"Shipmates, have you signed for that ship?"

Queequeg and I had just left the *Pequod* and were strolling down by the water, when we heard these words coming from behind us. We looked around until ours eyes rested upon the stranger dressed in rags. He asked the question again, "Have you signed for her?"

"The *Pequod*, you mean?" I responded.

"Aye, the *Pequod*," and he pointed to her. "Have you not got any fear? Aren't you afraid of Old Thunder?"

"Come on, Queequeg," I said, "let's go. This man's crazy; he doesn't know what he's talking about or who he's talking about."

"Stop! I'm talking about Old Thunder. You haven't seen him yet, have you?"

"Who's Old Thunder?" I asked.

"Captain Ahab."

"Captain Ahab! He's the captain of our ship," I exclaimed. "No, we haven't seen him yet. They say he lost his leg on his last voyage, but he's getting better and will be fine again soon."

"Not a chance! The day that Captain Ahab's fine will be the day that I'm a rich man!" the stranger laughed. "What else did they tell you about him?"

"Not much," I had to admit, "but they did say he's a good whale-hunter."

"That's true, that's true," he agreed, "but you haven't heard the whole story."

"Look, I don't want to hear the whole story. All I know is that he lost his leg."

"Don't want to hear more, eh? Well, you've already signed so you can't turn back now. Guess somebody's got to sail with him. Bless you, mates. Sorry I stopped you. Morning to you. Morning."

"Yes, morning to you," I responded glumly.

Queequeg and I then crossed the road and turned around to retrace our steps so that we passed the man on the other side of the road. Strangely enough, he did not even look our way. This relieved me and, after deciding that he was just a silly old man who was trying to scare us, I erased his words from my head.

Over the next several days there was great excitement aboard the *Pequod*. Old sails were mended and new ones were purchased. Bildad did all the buying from the stores while Captain Peleg stayed on the ship and kept a sharp lookout on the hands. Men were hired to work on the rigging—that is, all the ropes, chains, and cables connected with the masts and sails—and were seen on board well after nightfall. There were so many things to think of before the *Pequod* was set to sail. Imagine packing for a trip that couldn't make a visit to a grocery store, bank, or doctor for three full years. Our list of supplies was long enough to circle the equator! As we crossed each item off the list, our day of departure drew nearer. I thought that if Captain Ahab didn't soon appear, we would have to add the item "a new captain" to the list.

Queequeg and I often asked about Captain Ahab, and how he was, and when he was going to come on board the ship. In response, people always said that he was getting better every day and that he would arrive any time. I had to admit that I had a growing concern that I had not met the man who was to be our captain.

Finally, it was announced that the *Pequod* would sail some time the next day. Queequeg and I got to bed in good time that night in order to be well rested for our early rise.

It was six o'clock on a gray misty morning, when Queequeg and I neared the wharf. "Look, Queequeg," I exclaimed, "do you see that? It looks like some sailors running ahead to the ship. But maybe I'm wrong. It's hard to tell. We'd better go and find out. Come on."

Just then, "Halloa!" cried a voice from behind. We each felt a hand on our shoulders as a man forced his way in between us. It was the stranger we had seen the day we signed for the *Pequod*.

"Going aboard, are you?"

"Don't you dare touch us!" yelled Queequeg.

"It is none of your business whether we're boarding." I barked. "My friend and I are about to leave for the Indian and Pacific Oceans. Now, if you'll please excuse us."

But grabbing hold of our shoulders once again, he asked, "Did you see anything looking like men going toward that ship awhile ago?"

I was stunned by his straightforward question, and found myself answering, "Yes, I thought I did see four or five men, but it was very misty, you know. Now, please go."

"Misty, yes, very misty," he mumbled. "Just thought I might warn you, but never mind, never mind. Morning to you." And he was out of sight.

Deciding that we'd better hurry and find out what was going on we raced to the *Pequod*. Surprisingly, we found everything locked up and extremely quiet. The only human we discovered was a sleeping sailor below the decks. Queequeg and I decided that he should be questioned about the sailors I thought I'd seen earlier. The sleeper had made a bed out of a wooden chest and was sleeping face down across it. Queequeg put his hand on the sleeper's rear checking its softness, and then promptly sat down.

"Goodness, Queequeg, don't sit down there!" I shouted. "Get off. You're too heavy!"

Queequeg removed himself and, in doing so, woke the sleeper. The man knew nothing of the sailors we mentioned, but he did say that Captain Ahab had boarded the ship during the night. I wanted to ask him some questions concerning Ahab, but we were disturbed by the crew who had begun boarding the ship. Soon there was a lot of action with people bringing on last-minute things and I was unable to find out more about Ahab who must have been quietly tucked away in his cabin.

Toward noon, the word came from below that Captain Ahab was ready. The second mate, Mr. Stubb, called out, "Nothing more is needed from shore. Call all hands. Muster up the men. Away we go!"

And so, with no sign of Ahab, the anchor was lifted and the sails were set. The crew joined together in a hearty cheer as we plunged into the great Atlantic. It was a cold and damp Christmas Day.

Before I describe more of my venture in the whaling business, I'd like to take the time to talk a bit about the whaleman and whaling. You see, whaling has been given, by most landlovers, a very poor reputation. The whaleman is not honored as a doctor, lawyer, or teacher is honored. Most people think of the whaleman as nothing better than a filthy butcher.

Well, I have something to say about this! First, a whaleman may look a little dirty, but his ship is among the cleanest things on this earth. And as for being a butcher, yes, butchers we may be, but what commander in any war is not a butcher? And aren't commanders awarded medals and thought of as great heroes? For what, I ask you? For killing fellow humans, that's what!

Now, I'm not asking for medals, but do you not agree that the whaleman deserves some respect? After all, whale oil is the only fuel we have to light our lamps. Killing whales is necessary so that man does not have to live in darkness. And so, fellow men around the world, when you light your lamps tonight be sure not to insult the men who have given you this great gift!

I now return to the *Pequod* where I'll introduce to you its most honorable officers. The first mate was a native of Nantucket named Starbuck who had left a wife and child at home. Other than being extremely thin, he was not unattractive to look at. Starbuck was a responsible and dependable man of reason. If you looked into his eyes you'd catch a glimpse of his emotional strength. You'd see the painful memories and the calmness he used in dealing with them. But if you looked beyond his eyes deep into his soul, you would discover a deep inner fear. "I don't want a man in my boat," he said, "who is not afraid of the whale." He meant that anyone with no fear at all was worse than a coward (perhaps the word is "stupid"). Starbuck said that he was in the whaling business to kill whales and not to be killed by them, as his father had been, and his brother. It's no wonder that Stubb the second mate was heard saying, "Starbuck's the most careful whaler you'll ever find."

If you were looking for a complete opposite to Starbuck, it would be Stubb. Stubb was from Cape Cod and he was a carefree, reckless man who enjoyed each day as it came. He looked as cheery as a stout gentleman on a park bench puffing merrily on his pipe. How could anyone, especially on a whale ship, be so cheery all the time? Perhaps it was the pipe. A pipe somehow makes a man look cheery and Stubb was never seen without his short black pipe. It was part of his face. He was easy and cool even at the height of a whale killing when those monstrous jaws were open ready to snap. He'd casually scoop up his lance, whistle a few notes, puff a few puffs, and toss his weapon as if it were a stick

thrown for a dog to fetch. There was no fear in this man, at least not about death. He seemed to treat death like a pillow, something that he would some day lay his head on and rest comfortably forever.

The third mate was Flask, a native of Martha's Vineyard, an island off the coast of Massachusetts. Flask was a short stalky fellow with a fierce stubbornness. He acted as if the great whale was put on this earth as his number one enemy and he set about to destroy any of them that came his way. He killed whales for the fun of it —not very honorable, I admit—and looked upon them as nothing but oversized goldfish. His three-year voyage was simply a game of revenge. Flask had that fearlessness that Starbuck hated which made him—what was the word?—oh, yes: stupid. Nevertheless, Flask was an excellent whaleman.

Now these three mates were the headsmen of the three boats that were lowered from the main ship when it was time to make an attack on the whales. Just as Captain Ahab was captain of the main ship, these men were the captains of their own smaller boats. These boats were about twenty-five feet long and had oars as well as sails. They carried six men—five rowers plus the headsman. Of the five rowers, the one that sat in the bow was the harpooner. Because the harpooner and the headsman worked together as a team, it was important that they be carefully selected for each other.

First of all, Queequeg was chosen as Starbuck's harpooner. You already know Queequeg. Next was Tashtego, an Indian and a great hunter; he was to be Stubb's harpooner. Third among the three was Daggoo, a huge black man with such big golden hoops in his ears that we were afraid someone might tie the ropes of the sails to his ears instead of to the proper rings on the boat. This six foot five man, next to little Flask his headsman, looked

like a giraffe next to a porcupine. These six men were the leaders of the *Pequod's* crew, all of whom were led by the mysterious Captain Ahab.

For several days after leaving Nantucket, Captain Ahab was nowhere to be seen. It became a habit of mine every time I came up on deck to glance around for an unfamiliar face. Each time, I couldn't help but remember the things said by that eerie man on shore. Despite the fact that I was sure our ship had the best sea officers available, I still felt uneasy.

For the first few weeks following our departure from Nantucket, we experienced some cold polar weather. But as each day passed, we were going farther and farther south toward the equator, and we slowly left the weather behind us. On one of these more acceptable days, I climbed up from below and took my usual glance around. Shivers went through my spine. Captain Ahab stood on the deck no more than ten feet from me.

CHAPTER 5

Ahab's Mission

As I stood there on the deck facing Captain Ahab I realized that over the past days I had painted a picture of him in my mind that closely resembled a monster. Surprisingly, there was nothing horribly wrong with him despite his very gloomy manner. His large broad body seemed made of steel and he stood tall and steady glaring out into the sea. There was a determination in his glare that was unmistakable—as if to say: I'm ready for you. You're not going to beat me this time.

Looking closely, I noted a cluster of scars on his forehead making it look rough and wrinkled. Whether he was born with them or had been in some kind of an accident was hard to tell.

Being so entranced by the appearance of Captain Ahab, I almost forgot to look at his lost leg. I had been told by one of the crew members that his artificial leg was made from the ivory bone of the sperm whale's jaw. Captain Ahab stood with the end of his ivory leg in a hole that had been specially drilled about a half inch deep into the planks of the deck. Before long he returned to his cabin, but after that he was seen every day by the crew either standing with his leg in the hole, or heavily pacing the deck.

Around midnight several days after my first glimpse of Ahab, the crew was having trouble sleeping in their hammocks below. Just inches above their heads was the sound of Ahab's ivory heel crossing back and forth across the planks. Ahab was in the mood for heavy thinking and while doing his heavy thinking he was doing some heavy walking. Stubb, our easy-going second mate, took it upon himself to go up and tell Ahab that, although no one was going to tell him he couldn't walk the planks, could he please walk them a little more quietly. Ah! Stubb didn't know Ahab then.

"Do you think I can help it?" bellowed Ahab pointing to his ivory leg. "And anyway, who do you think you are telling me what to do. Get back to bed, you buffoon!"

For a second Stubb was silent and then he blurted out, "A buffoon? No one has ever said anything like that to me before, sir. You owe me an apology."

"Go!" said Ahab with great fury. "Go before I hit you."

"No, don't do that, sir," Stubb said politely. "Just a quick apology is all I'm asking."

"I will not apologize to you now or ever. In fact, I'll call you a buffoon, an idiot, *and* a jackass. And I'll kill you if you don't leave this instant!"

As he said this, Ahab made a motion as if to stab Stubb with his ivory leg. Stubb was filled with such terror that he decided it was time to retreat below the deck.

Descending into the cabin, Stubb found himself wondering what to do next, "Should I go back and fight him? Or should I lie here and feel sorry for the queer old man? He certainly is queer and so full of anger. There is something bothering him, that's for certain. Didn't Dough-Boy, the steward, say that when he goes to tidy Ahab's cabin in the morning, the bed is almost turned upside down? The pillow is at the wrong end, the sheets are twisted in knots, and his pajamas are soaked with sweat. He's a mixed up, queer old man alright. Ah, well, I could use some sleep."

In the morning, Stubb cornered Flask and told him what had happened the night before. "I don't know what to think," Stubb said, "but it's sure made me wiser, Flask. See Ahab over

there looking out into the water? Listen. Do you hear what he's yelling?"

"Look sharp, everybody!" shouted Ahab. "There are whales out there. If you see a white one, shout so all the world can hear!"

"Sounds weird to me, Flask," said Stubb. "A white whale? Something strange is going on."

Ahab's unusual behavior affected everyone on the ship. Up to this point in our voyage, we had been sailing in the deep blue waters but could still see land in the distance. For the next while, we would be lost in a great vastness and unable to see the shore. Somehow, losing complete sight of land made our unsure feelings toward Ahab grow stronger.

Let's put all uneasiness aside for the time being and have a look at some whale history. For ages, the Greenland, or right whale, was thought to be the king of the sea. It was considered to be the "right" whale to hunt because it was such a slow swimmer and so easy to catch. But, at the time of my story, a new king sat on the throne—the great sperm whale! Not only is the sperm whale the largest toothed whale and the deepest diver of all the whales, it is also the most valuable. A white, waxy substance called spermaceti is found in the sperm whale's head which is used in ointments and face creams. It was the sperm whale that we were after on this voyage.

You'll hear much more about the right whale further on in our voyage. In the meantime, we'll move on to a technical matter. The masts of a ship are the tall poles which support the sails and the mastheads refer to the top part of the masts. When on lookout, sailors stand on small platforms at the mastheads.

The *Pequod* had three mastheads which were manned twenty-four hours a day with the seamen taking regular turns every two hours. On a three-year voyage, the total num-

ber of hours you would spend at the masthead is about three months. That's twenty-four hours per day, times thirty days per month, times three months. Let's see, that equals two thousand-one hundred and sixty hours standing on a small piece of wood a hundred feet above the water. Being tossed about by the sea, the beginner feels like he is balancing on the head of a bucking bronco. And to think that straight down below swim vicious man-eating monsters just waiting for a tasty treat. I can tell you, however, after taking many turns up there, that once you get used to it, it can be very relaxing and peaceful.

While manning the masthead one morning after breakfast, I could see from my lookout that Ahab's continual pacing back and forth on the deck was leaving an interesting mark in the wood. The planks had worn down a darkened path that was dotted every three feet from his ivory leg. On this particular morning, Ahab followed the black dots with more purpose than ever before. All day long and into the evening his intense walking continued.

"Do you see him, Flask?" whispered Stubb. "He's wound up so tight that he's going to explode."

As if Ahab heard Stubb's words, he suddenly came to a halt and ordered, "Starbuck! Send everybody to the stern. The men at the mastheads, too. Quick!"

"But sir?" questioned Starbuck, who knew that this was a command used only in extraordinary cases.

"Do as I say!" shouted Ahab.

When the ship's entire crew was assembled at the stern of the ship, Ahab's eyes slowly inspected the group, and then strangely enough, he began pacing again. Not knowing how to react, the crew stood silent, worrying that this might go on forever. Fortunately it did not last long.

"What do you do when you see a whale, men?"

"Cry out for him!" was the chorus.

"Good!" cried Ahab. "And then what do you do?"

"Lower the boats and go after him!" shouted the men.

"And you don't quit until when?"

"Till he's dead, sir!"

What was so amazing to the crew was their growing excitement in answering such pointless questions. There was something about Ahab that stirred up in these men an eagerness that they themselves could not explain.

"All you mastheaders have heard me give orders about a white whale. Do you see this Spanish coin?" he asked, holding up the valuable piece of gold into the disappearing sun. "It's worth sixteen dollars, men. And it goes to the man who first sights a white-headed whale with a wrinkled forehead and a deformed mouth!"

Reaching for his hammer, he slowly rubbed the gold coin against his jacket to heighten its shine, and without a word, he nailed that coin to the mainmast.

"Hurrah! Hurrah!" cried the seamen.

"Remember, men, it's a white whale," began Ahab again. "You'll need a keen eye!"

Meanwhile, Tashtego, Daggoo, and Queequeg had listened with more seriousness than the rest. At the mention of the wrinkled forehead and deformed mouth, they each were reminded of something.

"Captain Ahab," said Tashtego, "that white whale must be Moby Dick."

"Moby Dick?" shouted Ahab. "Have you heard of him?"

"Is he quick to dive?" asked Queequeg excitedly. "And does he have an unusual humped back? And has he at least three harpoons in his side that are all... all... all..."

"Bent out of shape and mangled together!" bellowed Ahab. "Yes, mates, yes, it is Moby Dick you've seen!"

Suddenly, every man on the *Pequod* gasped. It all made sense—Moby Dick was the cause of Ahab's lost leg and the cause of Ahab's dark mood.

"Yes, my crew, it was Moby Dick that took my leg. That white whale is to be blamed for all my misery," Ahab almost sobbed. "But you are all here on the *Pequod* to help me get my revenge. This is my mission. And we can do it! Together we can kill that monstrous beast! We'll look all over the world if we have to, but in the end we'll find him. Oh, the joy in finding him! Now, men, are you feeling courageous? Are you ready for this? Are you?"

"Yes, yes!" roared the seamen—all but Starbuck who, standing back a little, was not captured by Ahab's evil magic.

"Are you with us, Starbuck?" asked Ahab.

"I came here to hunt whales, sir, not my captain's revenge. I'm on business, trying to earn a living, not out to be killed by a dumb white whale. This is insane!"

"Listen Starbuck," said Ahab calmly, "I am obsessed with that white whale. I see his horrifying strength and I hate it. I will punish him for it. Don't tell me it's wrong to chase the whale that destroyed me! I'd strike my own mother if she did the same! The crew, Starbuck, the crew is with me. See Stubb—he thinks it's all a big joke. Look at it as just another whale and money in your pocket, Starbuck. Side with us, or we're in for mutiny!"

Fearing this to be true, Starbuck murmured, "God help me. Help us all."

And with that, Ahab had the crew promise with all their soul to help him on his desperate mission. Long into the night they chanted, "Hunt and kill Moby Dick! Hunt and kill Moby Dick!"

CHAPTER 6

Thar She Blows!

Thinking back, I realize now that I was caught in Ahab's magical spell. I was one of that crew that shouted in favor of hunting Moby Dick. And the louder I shouted, the more I wondered if it was more out of a deathly fear of Ahab than of anything else. I had never heard of this white whale named Moby Dick and, therefore, did not fully understand the promise I was making. Now I was hungry to learn the legend of the whale that Ahab hated so much. And the crew was more than happy to satisfy my curiosity.

They told me that not all sperm whale fishermen knew of Moby Dick. Only a few had seen him, and an even smaller number had actually battled with him. The stories told by those who had encountered him were so frightening that even the bravest hunters shook in terror. It was said that at the sight of him, many sailors were so filled with panic that they dashed below the deck and refused to come up for days.

And then, of course, there was Ahab's tale. With his three boats and oars and men floating around him, Ahab had stabbed blindly at the white whale with his six-inch knife. His hope was to pierce deep enough to kill the whale. It was then that Moby Dick bit off Ahab's leg, as easily as a pair of scissors cuts a piece of thread. And it was then that Ahab blamed the whale for all the hatred he felt toward everyone and everything in this world.

As stories like Ahab's were told over and over again, I couldn't help but wonder if an amount of exaggeration was added to each telling. How else could I explain to myself why Moby Dick had become more of a man-eating monster with mysterious powers than a whale? Rumors claimed that Moby Dick had been seen at two opposite ends of the earth at the same time. How absurd that he could be in two places at once! Even more unbelievable were the stories telling how Moby Dick was pierced by several spears all at once and escaped unharmed. And then there were incidents when he spouted black blood, but then was seen spouting a normal water spray not too far away.

There was no doubt that Ahab's story greatly alarmed me. I knew that my life was in danger. But I was still confused about my feelings toward Moby Dick. I wondered when exactly Moby Dick chewed Ahab's leg off. Was it not *after* Ahab had stabbed him? Now if it were me that had just been stabbed, there's no telling what I might do! Was Moby Dick just acting in self-defense—you know, an eye for an eye, a tooth for a tooth? Here I found

myself puzzled over my feelings toward this giant fish.

I suppose there are people who would be appalled with the way I questioned the legend of Moby Dick. And I'm sure members of the crew would have thrown me overboard if they thought I was defending the whale in Ahab's story. I apologize for perhaps weakening the legend a little. Please don't misunderstand me. I do admit that Moby Dick was much larger and more fearsome than the normal sperm whale and that he had a very unusual wrinkled forehead and a deformed mouth. And I do agree that his uncommon whiteness definitely set him apart from other sperm whales. His appearance alone made him a legend—be sure of that!

I'm not sure how others felt, but of all Moby Dick's characteristics, it was his color that bothered me most. Even though white is often associated with things that are pleasant and pure, there is a peculiar emptiness about the color white. It is the emptiness of white that is more disturbing than even the bloodiness of red. Think of a ghost—do you not see a vision of whiteness? And if you've ever seen the dead, isn't the color drained from the skin and almost white? Yes, the whiteness of the white whale had me more upset than anything else.

I know my ramblings may about the white whale may seem exaggerated. But as Ahab's obsession became ours, our thoughts and our conversations dwelled almost constantly on Moby Dick. We watched and listened for the slightest warning of his approach.

"Shh! What was that noise, Cabaco?" whispered a man named Archy to his partner.

It was the middle of the night, and the seamen were passing buckets of water to fill the scuttlebutt, the ship's drinking fountain.

"Here, take the bucket, will you, Archy?" said Cabaco. "What noise do you mean?"

"There it goes again—under the deck—don't you hear it? It sounds like scratching."

"Nonsense. Pass me that other bucket."

"No—I hear it again!"

"Look. Your overalls are undone and the clasp is dragging on the deck. That's what you're hearing."

"No. Listen again."

And so the evening continued, back and forth, until Archy finally gave up the argument. But he knew himself that there must be someone, or something, down below hiding.

The following day was hot and muggy. The seamen were sluggish as they went about their duties. I was weaving a new coat for Queequeg—over and under, again and again went the yarn—when all of a sudden I was startled by a sound so bizarre and musical that I dropped the ball of yarn onto the deck. High above in the mastheads, Tashtego was peering excitedly into the horizon.

"Thar she blows! Thar she blows!" he cried. Instantly the ship was in commotion. There was no question that Tashtego had seen

sperm whales. The sperm whale shoots out its air on an angle that is easy to identify.

"There go the flukes!" reported Tashtego, meaning that the whales had dove and their tail fins had disappeared underwater. Sperm whales have been known to dive down with their heads pointing in one direction and then, while underwater, change direction. But we were sure that the whales had not seen us and would not be tricking us in such a way. We followed the path we were sure they were taking and, as expected, they surfaced just ahead of our ship. The sailors going in the smaller boats had gathered around while the three boats were swung over the sea on cranes.

At this crucial moment, a sudden cry was heard that caught everyone's attention. There stood Ahab, surrounded by five dark phantoms that seemed to appear out of thin air.

The five phantoms were loosening the ropes on a fourth boat that was supposed to be the spare. Ahab called, "Are you ready, Fedallah?"

Fedallah was tall and sunburned. He had an evil-looking tooth sticking out from his lips, and he wore a white turban coiled around his head like a snake. The rest of the group looked like natives from some island in the Philippines.

When Fedallah responded that his group was ready, Ahab shouted to the entire crew, who were still staring at the strangers, "Lower the boats, men!"

In answer to the roar of Ahab's voice, the men hopped over the rails and landed in their boats which were then lowered into the water. They had hardly pulled out from the ship when the fourth boat came around the back to join them. Ahab was clearly the headsman.

"Captain Ahab—?" cried Starbuck, who knew that the captain usually stayed on the ship during a whale chase. "What are you doing in there?"

Ignoring Starbuck's question, Ahab commanded, "Spread out, men! Four boats can cover more water."

"Yes, sir," agreed Flask. "Look, there ahead! There she blows! Archy, don't worry about those strange men over there; they'll make the job easier."

"Oh, they don't worry me, sir," said Archy, "I knew they were there all along. I told Cabaco about them the other night."

"Pull, men, pull," cried cheery Stubb to his crew who looked a little concerned. "Never mind those strangers—the more the merrier. We'll introduce ourselves later and share whaling stories. But for now, stroke, men, stroke until your muscles burst and your eyes pop out! Don't sleep on the job! Pull, will you? That's it—long and strong! Long and strong!"

Stubb had an unusual way of talking to his crew, but it worked. Oarsmen in Stubb's boat pulled for dear life! At this point, Stubb's boat neared Starbuck's and they were able to have a conversation.

"Mr. Starbuck, what do you think of those

mysterious newcomers?"

"Must be stowaways. Got on the ship somehow before we set sail. It's all very confusing, but never mind. There's money for us

all if we catch this whale. After all, that's why we're here, isn't it? To make a good profit."

"I suppose," agreed Stubb, "but the white whale's the reason for those men. Be sure of that!"

As for me, I silently remembered the man on shore who had seen the shadows boarding the ship just as I had that early misty morning.

Meanwhile, Ahab's crew was pulling like madmen and was ahead of the others. Fedallah, it appeared, was the harpooner. All at once, with oars in mid-air, everything stopped. The whales had apparently gone under and there was no movement on the water's surface telling where they might be. Sperm whales are easily frightened by sudden sounds; even the sound of an oar will cause them to dive. They eventually have to return to the surface, though, because whales need air. They are mammals, just like dogs, cats, and even you. And they must swim to the surface for a gulp of air after an underwater dive.

We would have to wait for anywhere between fifteen minutes and an hour and a half (that's the longest whales can hold their breath). Every man looked out into the area where the whales had been seen last.

Finally, Tashtego once again spotted the whales off in the distance. They had come up for air. After being underwater a long time, sperm whales hover just below the surface to ventilate their lungs. To you or any landsman, this would look like nothing but a little bit of bubbling water. To a whaleman, however, it marked the sign of whales. Tashtego cried, "There they are! After them, after them—let's go men!"

All four boats rowed frantically toward the whales while Starbuck, Stubb, and Flask shouted in chorus, "Pull, strong men, pull!" The chase was on.

In all the excitement no one noticed a storm developing or realized that the waves were curling and hissing around us like wild serpents. To make matters worse, the whales' spouting had caused a thick mist. The boats could no longer see each other or the ship. Somehow a group of whales found Starbuck's boat (the one I was in) and began to circle it. We were trapped in the center. Queequeg tried desperately to get close enough to the whales to throw his harpoon.

At last, we heard a short whooshing sound leaping out of our boat; it was Queequeg's harpoon. At once, all was chaos! Our boat was pushed and bounced from side to side as though giants were using it as a ball in a game of catch. And then, the game over, we were thrown out into the sea. While helplessly suffocating, we watched the harpooned whale escape. Queequeg had only grazed him.

Though we had been completely swamped, by some miracle our boat was unharmed. We swam around picking up our floating oars and then collapsed back into the boat. We called to the other boats, which were nowhere to be

seen. The wind grew to a wild wail and the
storm spun itself into a frenzy.

Bit by bit, the boat was filling with water.
It seemed we were doomed! At last, Starbuck
was able to light a lamp and attach it to the
end of a pole. He handed it to Queequeg who
stood like a man holding up his only hope in
the middle of disaster.

Soaked to the bone and shivering cold, we
were about to give up. It was dawn and we

still had seen no sign of ship or boat. Suddenly Queequeg stood up with his hand to his ear. We all heard the sound of a faint creaking that was coming nearer and nearer.

And so, floating on the waves, we found our ship and were saved.

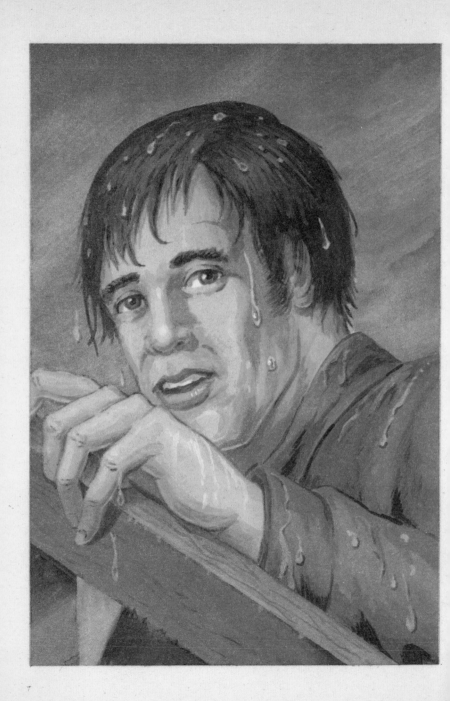

CHAPTER 7

An Interesting Gam

After our rescue, we learned that the other boats had turned back when the storm came. Although they were sure we were doomed, the ship cruised the water hoping to find a floating piece of evidence—a harpoon, an oar, or perhaps a hat.

There are times in our lives when we face the fact that we are going to die. My first whale hunt was one of those times. I know I had asked for danger, but I wasn't sure how many more times I could cope with this.

As they dragged me onto the deck and I was still shaking in my wet clothes, I said,

"Queequeg, my friend, is this really what whaling is all about?"

Acting as if it was just another regular work day, Queequeg nodded that, yes, it was quite normal. It was then that I learned about the sperm whale's habits. When they are frightened they swim in a circle so that they can look in all directions. The members of a group of sperm whales are very close. If one member is harpooned, the rest of the group comes to stampede the boat. I also learned that, in our case, we were very lucky that the whales backed off after capsizing our boat. It is quite common after an attack for a sperm whale to charge a boat with its jaws opened wide. I realized that the bare facts, with no amount of exaggeration, were horrifying.

Once all the excitement had died down after our first encounter with the whale, nobody seemed to question the phantoms. The crew decided they were castaways found floating in the open sea. It was not uncommon for a whale ship to pick up stranded sailors tossing about the sea on planks, oars, or bits of junk.

Time passed. The *Pequod* was making its way across the Atlantic Ocean and was heading south toward the tip of South Africa to the Cape of Good Hope. It was while sailing through these waters, that every night in the moonlight a whale was spotted. Because it is impossible to hunt whales in the dark, the men below were not wakened. Now, after our last episode, you'd think the crew would have been relieved. Not a chance! They were filled with eagerness for another chase. As the sightings continued, however, the crew began to wonder if the whale was none other than Moby Dick. And each time his flukes disappeared it was as if he were waving for us to follow him. The greatest fear, of course, was that Moby Dick would suddenly turn and charge our ship.

As the days lingered and we approached the Cape, the weather turned from a peaceful blue to a tortuous black. The winds howled as our poor boat rose and fell in the angry sea. Homeless seagulls clung to our masts as if our boat was all that the poor birds had left. Cape of Good Hope, was it called? I think a more suitable name might be the Cape of Torture.

Ahab's mood was as black as the weather. He rarely spoke to his mates, but stood with his ivory leg in his special hole watching the weather. He stood for so long that the snow and sleet glued his eyelashes together.

Once we arrived at the Cape of Good Hope, the weather subsided. The Cape and its surrounding water was the center of activity for all sea travellers. At this grand meeting place, we met the ship, the *Town-Ho,* from Nantucket, on its way home from a whaling voyage. What does a friendly, sociable whaler do when he meets another whaler in any sort of decent weather? He has a "gam." A gam is a social meeting between two whale ships. After they exchange hellos, the crews visit

each other and the two captains stay on one ship while the two chief mates go on the other.

We began our gam with the *Town-Ho* and, as it turned out, they had interesting news about Moby Dick. Two years ago, the *Town-Ho* had been cruising in the Pacific when one of the crew discovered that the boat seemed to have a leak down below. They figured that a swordfish had stabbed her. The crew had no luck finding the leak and, as the days wore on, it appeared to grow bigger. The captain decided to head for the nearest harbor to have the leak repaired. The breeze was strong and the *Town-Ho* would have easily made it to land if the following event had not occurred.

It so happened that there was an American named Steelkilt on the *Town-Ho*. Steelkilt was born and brought up on the wild ocean and had a temper that was just as wild. As long as he was treated with respect, however, he was completely harmless. Now it also happened that on the *Town-Ho* there was a mate named Radney. Radney was quite strict with his crew. And he did not show a decent amount of respect toward his men, particularly to Steelkilt. The situation was basically this: Radney did not like Steelkilt and Steelkilt knew it.

The captain had put mate Radney in charge of a group of pumpers whose job was to pump out the water from the leak. Steelkilt was one of those pumpers. So far, the *Town-Ho*'s leak required not much more than an hour a day of pumping. There were, however, some nervous mates who felt that even though only an hour was needed, the pumps should be going madly all day long. Radney was one of those mates. And, as I'm sure you have already guessed, Steelkilt was the type who felt that one hour a day was fine. It was only natural that each made the other mad and, well, you'll see what happened.

Steelkilt was sitting around, chatting with the other pumpers. Pretending not to notice

Radney who was approaching, he began, "Hey, my good friends! No need for more pumping today—unless, of course, Radney's scared that the boat's going to sink! What a fool he is!"

Ugly and mean, Radney decided that he would set about to pulverize the tall and noble Steelkilt into a heap of dust. Acting as though he hadn't heard Steelkilt's words, Radney shouted, "Why is the pump stopped? Get back to work!"

Being a hothead, Steelkilt jumped up and worked the pump like a man possessed. The men cheered as they listened to the gasping of his lungs. With a red face and sweat dripping down his nose, he finally stopped and sat down.

At that exact moment, Radney commanded that Steelkilt get a broom and sweep the deck. This request was amazing for two reasons. First, the deck was spotless and did not need sweeping and, second, this lowly job was meant for men not nearly as athletic as Steelkilt. There was no doubt that this was a great insult to Steelkilt, and he answered, "It is not my job to sweep the deck. I will not do it."

Radney grabbed a nearby hammer and shook it only several inches from Steelkilt's face. Furiously, he once again ordered Steelkilt to do the sweeping. At this point, Steelkilt rose slowly and spoke clearly, "I will not obey you and if that hammer so much as brushes my face I'll murder you."

Immediately, the hammer touched his cheek. In the next instant, Radney's lower jaw was crushed into his head and he fell on the deck gushing with blood. Steelkilt was, all of a sudden, surrounded by a group of Radney's men. Coming to the rescue, Steelkilt's comrades rushed in and pulled him free from his attackers. Before long, a brawl had begun.

The captain, upon hearing the commotion, arrived and ordered the scoundrel (meaning Steelkilt) to go to the bow of the boat. But Steelkilt and his men had no intention of obeying and they hid behind a blockade of barrels.

"Come out from behind there!" roared the captain while waving a pistol in each hand.

Jumping up on the barrels Steelkilt cried, "There'll be mutiny on this ship if I am murdered!"

Fearing this to be true, the captain made a deal. He put down the pistols and picked up a whip, saying, "If you return to your duties, I will not shoot you, but only give you a whipping."

"No deal!" shouted Steelkilt. "Promise not to touch us and then we'll go back to our work!"

"I make no promises—go to your duty, I say!"

"Captain, we can all leave this ship as soon as we arrive in the harbor. We don't want to fight. We want to work, but until we are treated decently and you promise not to whip us, we won't lift a hand," Steelkilt said calmly.

"Down into the hatchway then. I'll keep you there till you turn green."

Steelkilt's nine men were not happy, but they followed their leader down into the dark dungeon. As Steelkilt's head disappeared below the planks, the captain and his men padlocked the door and turned the key.

The captain ordered an all-night watch to be kept on the hatchway and twice every day for three days he asked the prisoners to come to work. Twice every day for three days they refused. On the fourth morning, when the hatch was opened, four men burst out ready to work. On the fifth morning three others gave in. Only three men were left.

"Would you like to come up now?" the captain said to the remaining men.

"Lock us up again, will you!" cried Steelkilt.

"Happily," said the captain, and the key clicked.

At this point, Steelkilt decided to form a plan. When the hatch was opened the next day, the three men would bolt out and take hold of the ship by running wildly all over the deck, flailing their long knives. The two others agreed that Steelkilt's plan was a good one. One thing that they did not agree on, however, was who should be the first man on deck. Steelkilt insisted that, being the leader, he should go first. Together these men had put up with so much misery, it's funny that a small

disagreement such as this could ruin everything. In the night, while Steelkilt was sleeping, his two companions bound and gagged
him and then called out for the captain.

Thinking a murder had taken place, the
captain opened the hatch and, not paying
attention to what the two men were saying,
grabbed all three of them and strung them up
side by side to the main mast. There the three
men hung until morning.

"You are so wretched the vultures wouldn't
even touch you!" cried the captain in the
morning. He then proceeded to whip the two
men, leaving Steelkilt to be dealt with last.
Removing the gag from Steelkilt, the captain
drew back his whip and said, "Let's hear what
you have to say for yourself."

"If you whip me, I'll murder you!" hissed
Steelkilt.

"You don't scare me!"

Then a strange thing occurred. Steelkilt
whispered something in the captain's ear that

no one else heard. Whatever it was, it caused the captain to put down his whip and say, "I can't do it—let him go. Cut down the rope."

No one knew what was said, but the men were lowered and everyone returned peacefully to their duties. Steelkilt told his men to behave until the ship reached land. They could abandon her then if they wished.

Now you would have thought that because of the leak, the *Town-Ho* would have stopped whale hunting—not so! The men were just as keen as before, especially Radney. With a bandaged head, the mate was desperate to take his anger out on a whale.

Though Steelkilt had told his men to behave, he was secretly planning a revenge against Radney. Knowing that Radney sat up all night, Steelkilt requested the night watch. He learned that Radney was in the habit of dozing off at one o'clock in the morning. Steelkilt planned a murder to take place in three days at that precise hour.

By some miracle, an event happened on the second day that freed Steelkilt from doing the bloody crime.

While the crew was washing down the decks, a man shouted all at once, "Thar she blows! What a whale! Look at the size of her."

It was Moby Dick. The ship went into a panic and the boats were lowered. As chance would have it, Radney's harpooner was Steelkilt and he got out ahead of the others and

harpooned Moby Dick first. Instantly, the boat hit something and Radney, who was standing up, was thrown out to sea. The boat drifted away, but Radney was left swimming helplessly with the whale. Almost immediately, the whale reared up so high that three quarters of his body was out of the water and, if you looked hard, you could see Radney's boots kicking wildly between the whale's teeth. In the next instant, the whale dove deep down into the water and Radney was never seen again.

The *Town-Ho* eventually landed and got her leak fixed, but most of the crew abandoned her. And where Steelkilt is right now, no one knows. It is said, though, that on the island of Nantucket, Radney's widow still cries when she looks out to sea and thinks of the dreadful white whale that killed her husband.

CHAPTER 8

Fine Dining
on the Pequod

S ome time had passed since our meeting with the *Town-Ho* and we were sailing across the Indian Ocean. This part of the voyage was not nearly as lively as other parts; there were fewer sightings of porpoises, dolphins, and flying fish. Being rather bored, and the hot weather not helping, the *Pequod*'s crew was unusually drowsy.

It was my turn to stand at the masthead and I was having difficulty staying alert. I was caught in a trance as I rocked back and forth to the beat of the waves below.

With a shock, I was brought back to life by the sound of bubbling water. An enormous sperm whale lay rolling in the water not two hundred feet away! So relaxed was he, spouting his water, that I thought he looked like a fat pig basking in the mud.

"Thar she blows!" I cried.

As if struck by a stone, the entire crew sprang into action. As the boats were being lowered, Ahab told the men to speak in whispers and not use their oars. The sails were set in our boats and we glided to our prize. Despite our quiet, the whale must have sensed danger. He lifted his tail forty feet in the air and then sank out of sight like a building being swallowed up in quicksand.

"There go the flukes!" was the announcement.

Stubb lit his pipe the instant the whale disappeared knowing that there would be a wait. When the whale surfaced, Stubb was closest and, still puffing on his pipe, cheered his crew on to the attack. By now the whale was full of terror and a powerful change had come over him. He was swimming "head out," which means that he had raised his head up out of the water. A whale's head is very light so it can be easily lifted up. When a whale goes head out he can swim very fast. It makes for an exciting chase.

At last, Stubb's command was heard, "Stand up, Tashtego! Give it to him!" and the harpoon was hurled.

In order for you to understand this scene and other similar scenes to come, I must tell you about the important, yet sometimes dangerous, whale line. One end of the line is attached to the harpoon and from there it winds back through the boat to where it is coiled in a tub. Boats can have as many as three harpoons with attaching lines and tubs. When a harpoon is thrown, the line begins to uncoil like a whip. This uncoiling happens so fast that smoke will rise from the tub. Even the smallest tangle or kink in the line while it is uncoiling can take somebody's arm, leg, or entire body off. The men had to be careful to stay clear of it.

The line is designed to help kill the whale in the following way: when the harpoon lodges itself in the whale's body, the fright and pain of it causes the whale to dive or sometimes take off at a frightening speed. The line uncoils and the boat is dragged behind, sometimes at an incredible speed. Next, the harpoonist at the bow of the boat changes places with the headsman at the stern. In time, the whale either comes up for air or grows tired from swimming and finally quits. All hands work toward pulling the boat to the whale, and when the boat is close enough, the headsman throws his lance. The lance is meant to pierce the lungs so that the whale bleeds to death.

Stubb and his men killed their whale exactly as I just described. When the whale was lanced, he rolled over and over in his own thick pool of blood. His spout hole opened

and closed as if he were gasping for air. At last, his heart collapsed and Daggoo said, "He's dead, Mr. Stubb."

Stubb dumped the ashes from his pipe into the water. He stared for a long time at the reddish water and ashes swirling together—death mixed with death. Finally, he organized the towing of the whale back to the ship. It took every man in the three boats all day to complete this task.

Heavy chains were used to tie the whale's head to the stern of the ship and his tail to the bow. Poor whale! He wouldn't have been happy to know that he was almost hugging the ship that belonged to his murderers.

It seemed that the sight of the dead whale brought about disappointment and aggravation in the captain. It was as though it reminded him that Moby Dick was still out there to be killed. We knew that no matter how many whales we brought back to the ship, only the corpse of Moby Dick would satisfy him. Ahab called out his last orders for the day and then went to his cabin and was not seen again until morning.

Unlike Ahab, Stubb was very excited. Not only was he feeling full of victory, but he was also looking forward to a tasty meal of whale.

Whale as a food—where shall I begin? At least three centuries ago, the tongue of the right whale was a delicacy in France. And starting in Henry VIII's time to this day, barbecued porpoises, which are a species of the whale, are considered fine eating. Eskimo doctors recommend raw strips of whale blubber, which is the fat under the skin, as a very nourishing food for infants. This reminds me of the Englishmen who long ago were left behind in Greenland by their ship and lived for months on scraps of leftover whale. The Dutch whalemen call these scraps which look like doughnuts "fritters" and consider them a treat. Believe it or not, the sperm whale's brains are a delicacy. The skull is broken with an axe and

two whitish balls are removed, mixed with flour, and cooked. They taste similar to calves' head which I'm sure you'll agree is wonderful.

Despite all these fine whale foods, the whale, in general, is not thought of as a meal for most respectable people. It is extremely rich and full of fat. And besides, there is just too much of it! Imagine sitting down to a slice of meat as long as your table—it's enough to take your appetite away!

Now Stubb was a man who didn't care a bit whether or not eating whale was respectable. To him, it was the best.

"Before I go to sleep I need a steak! Daggoo, go overboard and cut me one!" Stubb yelled.

It was midnight when that steak was cut and old Fleece, the cook, was wakened to prepare Stubb's meal. By the light of two lamps, Stubb ate his supper all alone. Well, not quite alone—thousands of sharks were also feasting on the whale. If you were to look overboard, you would see the sharks rolling over and over as they scooped out and fought each other for pieces of whale about the size of a human head. The men below in their bunks were kept wide awake by the loud thrashing of the sharks' tails against the ship. Above, Stubb grew annoyed with the noisy smacking of the shark's lips. To any man on deck, however, it was hard to tell which smacking belonged to Stubb and which to the sharks.

"Fleece, Fleece! Where are you?" cried Stubb. "Fleece, get over here!"

Already Fleece was not too pleased at being wakened at such a ridiculous hour to cook Stubb's meal. Being called once again by this outrageous second mate certainly did not improve his mood. He shuffled along until he reached Stubb and, with a great big sigh, stood with his arms crossed in front.

"Cook," said Stubb, lifting a very rare piece of meat to his mouth, "don't you think this steak is overdone? And you've made it too tender. Haven't I told you that I like my whale rare and tough? Just like those sharks over there. And what a racket they are making! Cook, go talk to them—tell them I'd be happy to share my whale, but they must keep quiet. Go now, Fleece, go give them a good talking to."

Fleece began, "Fellow animals: quit making so much noise! Do you hear? Stop smacking your lips! The mister says you're welcome to some meat, but stop all the noise!"

"Cook," interrupted Stubb, "you mustn't talk to them so mean. That's no way to get them to stop."

"You go talk to them yourself then, sir," Fleece said gloomily.

"No, Cook; try again. You'll do fine."

"Beloved fellow animals—"

"Good!" said Stubb. "That's it. That's the way to do it!"

"I don't blame you, fellow animals, for all that slapping," Fleece continued. "I know that's just the way you are. But please try to control your temper a bit. That's my point.

Because if you control your temper, you'll make old Stubb over there happy. And then you'd make me happy. And try to be polite while helping yourself to that whale. No need to be grabbing the blubber out of each other's mouths. Doesn't every shark have a right to that whale? And, by gosh, come to think of it, none of you really has a right to that whale! That whale belongs to Mother Nature."

"That's the way to teach them!" exclaimed Stubb. "Go on."

"Oh, it's no use, sir. Those beasts will keep attacking and slapping each other. They don't hear a single word I'm saying. No use talking to them until they're stuffed full and even then they won't hear because they'll sink to the bottom."

"Give them one last word anyway, Cook," said Stubb.

"Wretched fellow animals! Kick up the biggest fuss ever! Stuff yourselves till you burst and then roll over and die!"

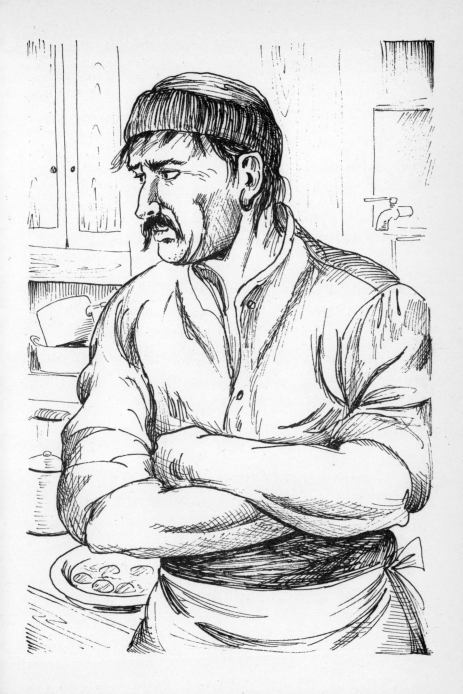

"Cook, come stand over here and pay attention," said Stubb. "That was a poor ending. Nevertheless, you may go."

But Fleece had hardly taken three steps, when Stubb's voice was heard again, "Cook, give me whale cutlets for supper tomorrow and ground whale for breakfast. Don't forget!"

Fleece thought to himself, "Sure wish the whale would eat him, instead of him eat the whale." And with that, he went back to bed.

Realizing that if the sharks were left to feast on the whale, there would be nothing left by morning, Stubb called upon Queequeg to deal with the mob of sharks.

Using a sharp tool similar to a garden spade, Queequeg leaned over the railing and began piercing as many shark skulls as he could. In all the confusion, sometimes he missed his target and the sharks were just tickled. This made them even more ferocious. They not only attacked each other, but bent themselves around and bit their own tails.

After almost losing a hand to one of the sharks, Queequeg said, "Whoever made the shark must have been someone pretty mean and ugly."

It was a Saturday night, and in the morning the process called the "cutting in" would begin. The *Pequod* would become a butcher shop and every crew member a butcher.

CHAPTER 9

The First Bad Sign

T he *Pequod* was ready for the cutting in. The first job was to behead the whale. Even to the most skilled whaleman, this is no easy task. When you look at a whale, there is no skinny neck; in fact, it is quite the opposite. Unfortunately, where the head and body meet is the thickest part of him. To make matters worse, the whaleman doing the cutting must work eight feet above the whale who is bouncing about in rough water.

Stubb was chosen to be the *Pequod*'s surgeon. And so, blindly, he worked to cut the whale exactly between the skull and the spine. How amazing that only ten minutes after he had begun, Stubb brushed his hands together and announced that he was done. The crew stared in astonishment at their most remarkable second mate. Once cut off, the head was left dangling at the stern of the ship to be dealt with after the cutting in was finished.

The next step was to set up two systems of hardware. Each system consisted of a pulley and a rope with a hook on the end. The hooks were called blubber hooks and weighed several hundred pounds each. The crew hoisted the hooks up to the main masthead and then swung them directly over the whale.

When everything was in place, Starbuck and Stubb leaned over the railing and cut a hole in the whale's back. Then one of the hooks was fastened in the hole. Together in song, a group of men began to heave on the rope. Suddenly, the boat leaned on her side, shook and trembled until at long last the men heard a great big snap. With a swish, the boat bounced upright, and the hook was seen dangling in the air dragging behind it the first strip of blubber. The men continued heaving until the blubber reached the masthead and could go no further.

Next, Tashtego sliced the blubber from the body. Immediately, this strip of blubber, which was now called the blanket piece, swung freely from the hook. (Blanket piece, by the way, is a very fitting name because the whale is wrapped up in his blubber like an Eskimo wrapped up in his blanket. It works like a blanket, too, keeping the whale warm in even the coldest temperatures.)

The blanket piece was now ready for lowering and the men, once again, began their song. Down through the hatchway, the blanket piece was lowered into the blubber-room. Here, many hands were working to cut the blanket piece into blocks and then slice it into bacon-like strips called Bible leaves. What was done with the blubber from this point will be told later on in my story.

Meanwhile, the second hook was inserted in the whale where a new hole had been cut. While the first blanket piece was lowered by one group of men, the next strip of blubber was raised by another group. This process was repeated until all the blubber was removed from the whale. The blubber of a whale is much like an orange rind. Just as an orange spirals when it is peeled, a whale rolls over and over in the water as the blubber is stripped off its body.

Again and again, the process was repeated with the hooks being raised and lowered, the mates cutting, the ship rocking, the crew singing, the men in the blubber room slicing, and all bodies sweating miserably in the wicked heat.

When the final tasks of the cutting in were finished, the whale's skeleton was cut loose. As the empty bones grew smaller and smaller out the back of the ship, a whale ship was spotted growing larger in the front. Since it was still too far away to be able to catch, the *Pequod* decided to send out a signal and see what kind of an answer she would get.

All ships have private signals which are collected in a book. This helps boats recognize each other on the ocean from great distances. The *Pequod*'s signal was at last answered and we were able to conclude that the ship was the *Jeroboam* of Nantucket.

A boat had been lowered from the *Jeroboam* and was heading toward the *Pequod*.

Starbuck ordered that a ladder be lowered so that the two ships could have a gam. As this was being done, the captain in the boat waved his hands to suggest that the lowering of the ladder was not necessary. It turned out that the *Jeroboam* had a horrible contagious disease on board and that Mayhew, her captain, was afraid of spreading it to the people on the *Pequod*.

This by no means stopped the two captains from having their gam. The oarsmen in the *Jeroboam*'s boat worked hard in the wavy sea to keep close to the *Pequod*. Pulling one of the oars in the *Jeroboam*'s boat was a young man with a face full of freckles and eyes that had a crazy look in them.

Stubb and I were standing next to each other a distance from the two captains. Stubb, eyeing the strange oarsmen, leaned over and whispered in my ear, "That's him! That's the man the *Town-Ho*'s second mate told me about. He was one of their crew!"

As it turned out, this man had been a cowardly fool on the *Town-Ho,* but as a crew member of the *Jeroboam,* he had a mysterious power over almost everybody on the ship. Stubb said that he was insane. When I asked why Captain Mayhew would ever let an insane man on board, he told me that this fellow must have behaved himself just before the *Jeroboam* departed from land.

Anyway, almost immediately after the *Jeroboam* set sail, this crazy man announced that he was a great prophet—a man who thinks he can predict the future. He told the crew that he controlled the sea and all that happened on it. His imagination never rested and he terrorized the crew with threats of what would happen if they did or didn't do this or that. The crew, not knowing any better, began to think of him as some marvelous god.

This dishonest man refused to do any of the ship's work and the Captain wanted to get rid of him by dropping him off at the nearest port! But the crew wouldn't hear of it! They said they'd all desert the ship if their prophet left. The captain, therefore, was forced to keep the man on board.

Since the disease broke out, this crazy man had more power than ever. He claimed that he controlled the disease and those who didn't obey him would get sick and die. The sailors bowed down before him and did whatever he asked.

All of a sudden, I heard Ahab say something that caught my attention, "Have you seen the white whale?"

Before Mayhew could answer, the prophet jumped to his feet, shouting, "Beware! I say, beware of that hideous whale with his hideous tail!"

Ignoring the man, Mayhew began a disturbing tale about *Jeroboam*'s adventure with Moby Dick. (Needless to say, our foolish prophet was excellent at interrupting!) The tale went something like this:

When the *Jeroboam* first set sail, the prophet had warned the captain that he should under no circumstances attack the white whale. (You see, the prophet was deathly afraid of Moby Dick.) A year or two later, when Moby Dick was sighted from one of the mastheads, Macey, the first mate, was itching for a chase. The captain agreed he should be allowed to go even though the prophet said, "Sail on!"

Macey convinced five men to join him and they pushed off in their boat. After a lot of hard work, a harpoon was finally lodged. Meanwhile, the prophet was standing at the masthead frantically waving his arms and screaming that the men were heading for doom. Macey, now standing in the boat's bow, was trying to throw his lance. Suddenly, a huge white tail rose into the air and then smacked down on the water. In the next instant, Macey was tossed across the sea as though he were following a rainbow's path. Not a plank on the boat was scratched, but the mate sank and was gone forever.

Our prophet saw it all and convinced the rest of the terrified crew to call off any further hunting of the whale. Of course, this tragic event only made the prophet look even more wonderful. The crew was sure that he had known all along exactly what was going to happen to Macey.

Having concluded his story, Mayhew asked whether Ahab was planning to hunt the white whale. Ahab told him he most certainly was, at which point the prophet jumped to his feet and shouted, "Remember the dead Macey down there! Remember what happened to him!"

Showing no emotion, Ahab said to Mayhew, "Captain, I've just thought of a letter we received. I'm sure it's for one of your officers. Starbuck, look in the bag."

Every whale-ship collects letters for other ships. But those letters can only be delivered if, by some small chance, the two ships meet up somewhere in the watery world. Unfortunately, most letters do not reach their destination and, if they do, they are often about three years late.

In no time Starbuck returned with the crumpled damp letter in his hand. It had green spots of mold on it.

"Give it to me!" ordered Ahab and he began trying to make out the faded scribbling on the envelope. "It says, Mr. M - A - C - ... now let's

see . . . oh, I know, Mr. Macey, Ship *Jeroboam*. That's what it says. But, by gosh, he's dead!"

"Poor Macey! And it's from his wife," sighed Mayhew. "Let me have it!"

"No," cried the prophet to Ahab, "keep it yourself. You can give it to the dead man yourself. You'll be seeing him soon."

"Quiet, you! I'm going to live to see Moby Dick killed!" shouted Ahab and then he pierced the letter with the end of a harpoon and stretched it out toward Mayhew. But, just then, the boat drifted a little so that the harpoon was pointing right at the prophet's nose. He grabbed the harpoon with its attached letter, spun it around like a baton, and hurled it back in our ship. It landed at Ahab's feet. The prophet shrieked at the oarsmen to row and the boat shot away rapidly from the *Pequod*.

As the men on the *Pequod* went back to their work, they couldn't help thinking that the letter that ended up in their boat was a bad sign of things to come.

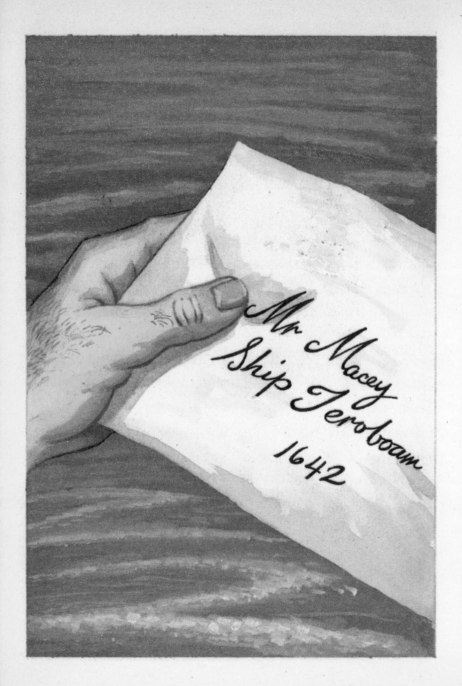

CHAPTER 10

Hanging Heads

There is still more to be said about the business of cutting in. I'd like to retrace our steps a little, back to where the first blubber hook was inserted into the hole dug out by Starbuck and Stubb. Perhaps I should first apologize for jumping around in my description of the cutting in. Then again, perhaps I shouldn't apologize. Jumping around was exactly what the crew did when they were cutting in. No one was standing still; there was so much running back and forth. Jobs to be done here, jobs to be done there, and all at the same time. And so I think my jumping around has given you the true flavor of cutting in.

Where was I? Oh, yes: inserting the first blubber hook. You must have wondered how that huge hook was fastened in the hole on the whale's back. It was put there by our friend Queequeg whose job it was as a harpooner to climb on the whale's back and attach it. The whale, I might add, was lying almost entirely under water. The harpooner had to stay on the whale until the whole stripping process was complete. Do you recall that I described the stripping of the whale's blubber like the peeling of an orange? Thinking of that, you'll understand how difficult it was for Queequeg, who was ten feet below the deck, to keep his balance on a spinning dead whale's back.

Being Queequeg's dearest companion, it was my duty to help him stay on his feet and I used something called a "monkey rope." Have you ever seen a puppeteer work the strings of a marionette to make it dance? I was the puppeteer and Queequeg the doll. Instead of strings we used the monkey rope. The monkey rope had a canvas belt at each end: one to go around Queequeg's waist and the other to go around mine. We were joined together by the rope.

Just as a puppeteer and his doll are a team, so were Queequeg and I. We were completely committed to each other. That meant that if Queequeg lost his balance and sank, it was my duty to be pulled under with him. There were times when I had to yank poor Queequeg hard to stop him from getting jammed between the whale and the ship. On the other hand, there were times when he jerked me so suddenly that I almost came flying overboard.

To make the situation worse, the sharks Queequeg had attacked during the night had returned. They swarmed around the whale like ants on an anthill. And they were thirsty for more blood. Right in the middle of those hungry sharks was Queequeg who pushed them away with his dancing feet.

I must stop for a minute. I am sure you must think I am exaggerating. Why wouldn't the sharks eat Queequeg in an instant? Amazingly enough, if there is a dead whale to feast on, a shark will not go after a human. I suppose to a shark, a whale is like sirloin steak and a human is like liver. Now, which would you choose?

You'd think that this situation couldn't get much worse. Well, it did. Just because a shark prefers whale does not mean that if a human is dangling right in front of his nose the shark will pass him by. It is still very wise to be careful. Tashtego and Daggoo decided they wanted to do their part in protecting Queequeg. Using their sharp harpoons, they leaned over the railing and slaughtered as many sharks as they could. This was very good of them and they did mean well. But I must say, it was rather dangerous for Queequeg. In the bloodied water and all the confusion, it was hard to

tell which was a shark and which was Quee-queg. Poor Queequeg! What a sad state he was in—the sharks were his enemies and the harpoons were his friends and both were as dangerous as the other.

At last it was all over and Queequeg was lifted up on deck soaked and shivering. I pat-ted him on the back and told him how coura-geous he was, and then Dough-Boy handed him a cup of hot ginger and water.

Overnight and into the next morning, the *Pequod* drifted into water that had brit float-ing on it. Brit is a yellow substance that is the main food of the right whale. It was a good clue that some right whales were in the area. We were surprised because right whales were seldom seen anymore in this part of the world. I spoke before of the right whale and mentioned that it was the first whale that was ever hunted. Long ago, there were thousands of right whales all over the world. Unfortu-nately, they had been hunted so furiously that, at the time I was on the *Pequod*, they were disappearing rapidly.

The oil from a right whale is not nearly as valuable as the sperm whale's oil. For this reason, when Ahab announced that we would capture a right whale that day, the crew was surprised.

"Why do you think old Ahab wants a worthless right whale?" asked Stubb.

"Because that spooky Fedallah told him that if a ship has a sperm whale's head hanging on one side it should have a right whale's head on the other," answered Flask.

"Why?"

"I don't know. Supposedly it's good luck. Fedallah seems to know all about superstitions at sea. But if you ask me, he's nothing but trouble, and I think *he's* more bad luck than anything."

"He's trouble all right. And with that snake-looking thing on his head, he looks like the devil himself. Some night, if I ever get the

chance when no one is looking, I'm going to push him overboard, Flask. Yes, I am!"

"But if he's the devil, Stubb, why bother pushing him overboard? You know you can't kill the devil."

"I'd just like to give him a good dunking, that's all," answered Stubb.

"But what if he decided to dunk you? You'd drown. What then?"

"I'd like to see him try it! Do you know what I'd do? I'd grab the end of that turban and pull so he spun like a spool of thread on a sewing machine! Oh, no, I'm not afraid of the devil."

"Okay, okay, but why do you think Ahab likes him so much?" asked Flask.

"Do you know what I think, Flask? I think they've made a deal."

"A deal? What about?"

"You know how badly Ahab wants that white whale? Well, Fedallah is going to get it for him in exchange for Ahab's gold ring, or maybe even in exchange for something greater, like half of Ahab's entire fortunes."

"Come on, Stubb! Fedallah can't get Moby Dick himself."

"You never know with the devil," said Stubb.

Upon that conclusion, the two men were called to lower their boats and follow the right whales. In a short while, the men at the mastheads could only see two small specks on the water. But suddenly they saw splashes of white water followed by the two boats being towed by whale.

The harpooners in both boats had thrown their harpoons at the same whale. And both were being madly towed by the fleeing creature. This was not unusual. Sometimes more than one boat will harpoon the same whale because there is no guarantee that a thrown harpoon will lodge in a whale's back. Harpoons are often thrown from several boats in hope that at least one will lodge. And then, of course, there is the possibility that all the harpoons will lodge and all the boats end up being towed by their lines.

The whale was heading toward the ship pulling Stubb and Flask's boats! It looked as if the whale was going to smash us to bits! Just in time, he dove under. The whale had missed us, but Stubb and Flask were still being pulled toward the ship.

"Cut! Cut the lines," cried the nervous crew.

Stubb and Flask still had plenty of line left, and the whale was not diving too deep or too fast. They ignored the cries and held on. For a few minutes, it was a terrible struggle trying to direct the boats away from the *Pequod*. The two mates pulled this way and that, until finally their boats were free from danger. The crew members watching from the *Pequod* wiped the sweat from their brows.

After that, the killing of the whale went smoothly and the men towed the dead whale to the ship. Everyone was relieved that it had not been the other way around, that is, the whale towing dead men to the ship!

Just as Ahab wanted, now we had a right whale's head on one side of the ship and a sperm whale's head on the other. And in between, the crew laid their heads down for a well-earned rest. It had been a busy day.

With the two heads hanging over the *Pequod*'s side, how easy it was for me to compare them. All I had to do was walk from side to side across the deck. It hit me then how different they are. Even though both are enormous, about one-third the length of the body, the sperm whale's head has more personality. There is something about it that is says, "I am by far the superior."

The eyes of the two heads are basically the same: very small and quite low down on either side near the jaw. Because a whale's eyes are so far around the side, it cannot see anything that is exactly in front of him, unless it is very far away.

Very simply, his eyes are in the same position as your ears. Imagine seeing out of your ears. If your worst enemy was sneaking straight toward you, you wouldn't be able to see him!

Do you remember in the squall when our boat capsized and I said that the whales swam in a circle around us? That's what they have to do in order to see all around them. Needless to say, the position of the whale's eyes gives the whale hunter a tremendous advantage.

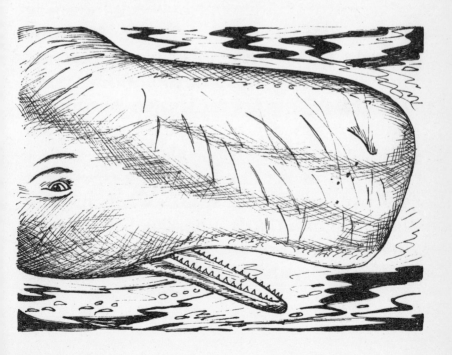

The ears of a whale are as interesting as its eyes. The ears are so small that you could search all over the head for hours and never find them. They have no flap and the holes are barely big enough to stick a needle through. But lucky for a whale, his ears are very sharp and make up for his awkward eyesight.

It's amusing to think of the huge, fearsome whale having eyes and ears more suited to a newborn baby. A baby is so innocent!

The greatest difference between the sperm whale and the right whale's head is the shape. The right whale's head looks like the toe of a boot (large enough, mind you, to fit a good-sized giant). The sperm whale's head is the shape of a rounded rectangle. When a sperm whale swims on his back, imagine his head as a large toy box. The lower jaw opens and shuts like the lid on the box. When an angry whale makes an attack on this back, whales can't see him coming because his head is underwater. And then, from out of nowhere, his jaw snaps. Many times a whale has bitten a boat in half this way.

There is no doubt that the snapping of a whale's jaw is more horrifying than anything I can think of. But if it were possible to stop the action and look inside, a whale's mouth is amazingly beautiful. It looks as though it is lined from top to bottom with shiny white satin. And along the outside, grand ivory teeth stand solidly in two rows.

It is the teeth that were being removed a few days after the cutting in. Queequeg, Daggoo, and Tashtego unhinged the lower jaw and hauled it onto the deck. One by one, they cut the whale's gums and dragged the forty-two teeth out of the mouth with ropes, like workhorses dragging boulders across a field.

CHAPTER 11

A Kill
for Nothing

To proceed in my story, I must continue with the sperm whale's head. The top part of the whale's head is known as the great Heidelburgh Tun. The Heidelburgh Tun runs the entire length of the whale's head and, on a good sized whale, that equals about twenty-six feet. The Tun contains by far the most precious oil in the sperm whale, the spermaceti. Do you recall how exact Stubb had to be in beheading the whale? If the Tun is accidentally punctured, the spermaceti can leak out and be lost.

Tashtego was given the task of removing the valuable liquid from our sperm whale's

Heidelburgh Tun. The first step was to sus-
pend the head high in the air by two hooks.
Then, agile as an acrobat, Tashtego made his
way onto the top of the whale's head. Using a
small sharp spade, Tashtego carefully searched
for the proper place to pierce the Tun. He
tapped all over the Tun like a builder tapping a
wall listening for the sound of the studs. At
last he waved to the crew down below to say
he'd been successful.

Using a rope and pulley, the crew set up
something that was much like a bucket in a
well. Two men on deck hoisted the bucket up
to Tashtego, who then used a very long pole to
push and guide the bucket deep down inside
the Tun until it disappeared. When Tashtego
gave the signal, the two men raised the bucket
up out of the head. It reappeared filled with a
liquid like a pail of thick white paint. Slowly,
the filled pail was lowered until it was caught
by a pair of hands that emptied the liquid into
a large tub. This process continued over and

over again until a second, and then third, tub was filled. As the Tun slowly emptied, Tashtego had to push his pole down harder and deeper. He struggled to keep his balance.

Tashtego was filling the eighteenth or nineteenth bucket when, all of a sudden, a strange accident happened. Somehow—my goodness, poor Tashtego!—he fell head first into the great Heidelburgh Tun and vanished! All we heard was a terrible gushing and swallowing sound.

"Tashtego's fallen!" shouted Daggoo, who reacted before anyone. "Quick! Swing the bucket over!"

"Stick your foot in the bucket and grab hold of the rope," ordered Starbuck. "We'll hoist you on top of the whale's head."

"Look!" cried the crew. "The whale's head is coming alive!"

It truly looked like it was. With Tashtego kicking furiously inside, the head appeared to be breathing heavily as if in a panic, too.

Daggoo, however, remained calm and continued with the rescue.

Suddenly, one of the two hooks holding the head snapped, leaving the entire weight held by only one hook. The second hook seemed ready to give way at any moment. Daggoo continued. He rammed down the bucket into the collapsed head hoping that Tashtego would grab it and be lifted out.

"Give up, Daggoo, give up!" begged the crew.

"You'll go down with the head. Climb down, Daggoo. Fast!" urged Starbuck. But Daggoo had kept a foot in the bucket and a hold on the rope. He knew that if the head fell he'd be held up safely in the air.

Just then, with a thunderous crash the head went tumbling into the sea. Daggoo was indeed held in the air by the bucket, but Tashtego was in a horrible state: alive and sinking to the bottom of the sea in a whale's head! In the next instant, courageous Queequeg dove in the water with a sword in his hand. Every man on the ship held his breath. I prayed that this wouldn't be the end of my dear friend Queequeg.

"Yahoo!" cried Daggoo who was still perched up above. "I see them! I see both of them!" The crew cheered joyfully as they watched Queequeg swim with one hand and drag Tashtego by the hair with the other. Both men were hauled up on the deck.

How, you may ask, did Queequeg free the trapped Tashtego? While diving after the slowly falling whale, Queequeg made swift slices with his sword near the bottom of the head. In no time, he had carved out a large hole into which he stuck his hand and yanked Tashtego out by the head.

It took some time for the crew to recover from the excitement of Tashtego's dreadful fall, but before long, even more excitement was brought on by an encounter with the German ship *Jungfrau*. Long ago, the Germans were the greatest whaling people in the world, but at the time of my story, they were rarely seen and no longer the greatest.

For some reason, the *Jungfrau* seemed unusually anxious for a visit. The captain, Derick De Deer, looked very impatient as he pulled up to the *Pequod* in his smaller boat.

"What's that in his hand there?" asked Starbuck.

"It looks like a coffee pot, Starbuck," answered Stubb.

"That's no coffee pot," laughed Flask. "It's an oil can! They've run out of oil!"

It does seem rather odd, doesn't it, for a whaling ship to run out of oil. Rather like a dairy farm running out of milk.

The minute the captain stepped on the *Pequod*'s deck, Ahab ignored the oil can and asked, "Have you seen the white whale?"

"No. Haven't seen him," answered Derick, "but could you spare some oil? It's been a while since we've made a kill and we're all out."

"Haven't seen Moby Dick, eh?"

"Not a sign of him. About the oil...," but before he could finish, Ahab had disappeared to his special spot on the deck.

Starbuck kindly filled Derick's can and the German captain departed gratefully. On his way back, whale were spotted from the mast-heads of both ships. Derick was so keen on getting a whale that, without even stopping to put his newly filled oil can on board, he turned and began a chase for oil of his own. Soon, three other German boats joined him and, by the time the *Pequod* had lowered her boats, the Germans had a big lead.

There were eight whales in the pod we were after and they were swimming furiously side by side. All but one. Lagging far behind the others was a huge old and deformed sperm whale. His breathing, or shall I say spouting, was weak and slow. Suddenly, the old whale heaved and rolled over in the water.

"Look at that fin!" shouted Stubb. "That's why he's so slow. It's nothing but a stump."

"I wonder if he was born that way or if he lost it in a battle?" I asked.

"Hang on, old fellow. I'll give you a splint for that injured arm," laughed cruel Flask, pointing to his harpoon.

"Better hurry," yelled Starbuck, "or the German will beat you to it."

By this time, the *Pequod*'s boats had passed three of the German boats. Derick's boat was still in the lead. But at the rate we were going, there was no question that we would pass him, too. In the meantime, we were worried that he'd soon be close enough to throw his harpoon and beat us to the whale. As for Derick, he seemed quite certain that this was exactly what would happen. He even had the nerve to shake his oil can at us, as if to say, "I don't care how nice you were, this whale is mine!"

"You ungrateful swine!" yelled Starbuck. And with that, all three mates picked up their speed, more determined than ever to beat the German.

Unfortunately, Derick had begun with such a big head start that it was looking as though he would indeed win. But as luck would have it, a crab landed on the oar of Derick's middle oarsman. The man reached over to pull the crab off and, because he was rather fat, Derick's boat almost capsized. Derick lost some time. Starbuck, Stubb, and Flask were still behind, but only by a little.

What a pitiful sight! The poor whale, being chased by the four raging boats, was beating his shortened fin against his side in fright. He struggled to keep himself balanced in the water but, like an injured bird trying to fly, was unable to steady himself.

All of a sudden, Derick stood up to take aim. In the next instant, the three Nantucketers jumped to their feet and sent their three harpoons sailing over the German's head and into the whale's back. Our harpoon was the only

one that successfully lodged. We were dragged by the whale right into Derick's boat. The German captain and his stunned crew were thrown overboard.

Watching the scene, Stubb cried, "Don't be worried, you animals. You'll be picked up soon—I saw some sharks heading this way."

The whale dragged our boat briefly before he dove down. So far down did he go that our line had completely run out. The nose of our boat was touching the water while our rear was high in the air. If the whale went down any farther, we would be have to cut our line or go under with him. Such a thing is quite common.

"Get ready, men. I think he's rising," said Starbuck.

Our nose gave a sudden bounce upward, and we began hauling the dripping rope back in our boat as quickly as we could. Soon the whale reached the surface. He was bleeding heavily and plainly exhausted. It was easy to lance him. I noticed that his eyes had horrible growths on them that looked like a fungus growing on a tree. My heart sank at the sight of him—so old, with only one arm and almost blind. Quickly, I shook myself from my feelings of sympathy, knowing that he must die so that men could light their lamps.

With great effort, we towed the whale and chained him to the side of the ship. During the cutting in, we found a lance head of stone buried in the blubber, that must have been older than even America. Who knows what other discoveries we might have made if we didn't have to let the fish go. Because he was so heavy and refused to float, he was causing the *Pequod* to tip over.

"Blasted whale! Will you stop sinking?" Stubb cried to the body.

"It's no use," I said as the chains were cut. "He's gone. What a waste. What a terrible waste!"

Shortly after we let the whale go, we heard a cry from our mastheads. At first our men thought they had spotted another group of sperm whales but, looking more closely, they realized that the whales were fin-backs. Sperm whales and fin-backs have similar spouts and can easily be confused by an amateur. There would be no chase because we knew that fin-backs are fast swimmers and almost impossible to catch.

Off in the distance, however, our men saw the *Jungfrau* lowering her boats again. Captain Derick must have been fooled by the spouts and, once again, was off on another useless hunt.

CHAPTER 12

Another White Whale Tale

The *Pequod* had crossed the Indian Ocean and was heading up toward the coast of Japan to our final destination, the Pacific Ocean. We would enter the Pacific in time for the great whaling season there. Ahab counted on finding Moby Dick in the Pacific—the ocean where Moby Dick was most frequently sighted. Besides, it was the last whaling ground left for us to search.

It was a week or two after meeting with the *Jungfrau* when the many noses on the *Pequod* smelled something very unusual and offensive. Looking around, we saw in the distance a French ship with a whale chained to her side. The vultures hovering over her like a big black cloud were a good clue that the whale was rotting. More than likely, it had been sick and the ship found the whale dead floating on the water. Can you imagine the amount of foul smell coming from a sick rotting whale?

The quality of the oil taken from a sick whale is extremely poor. There is only one good reason why a ship might bring in a sick whale and not every seaman is aware of the reason. The sickness may have been caused by a soft, sweet-smelling, waxy substance called ambergris found in the whale's stomach. Ambergris is as valuable as gold and is used to make perfumes, powders, and air fresheners. It certainly is hard to believe that something causing a whale to get sick would be valuable. And it is even more difficult to believe that something smelling so heavenly could come from such a foul-smelling beast. However strange it all may seem, what I say is true.

Stubb, being the sneaky man he was, developed a plan. If he could fool this ship into thinking the sick whale was worthless, he might be able to get the ambergris.

Calling for his boat, he went to meet the stranger. As he approached the ship, he was able to read her name in large shiny letters: *Bouton de Rose.*

"Rosebud?" said Stubb to himself. "What a funny name for a ship with such a dreadful smell!"

He called out to the first mate, "Have you seen the white whale?"

"What whale?" was the reply.

"The white whale, you know, Moby Dick? Have you seen him?"

"Never heard of him. No, sorry."

Stubb thought that this was a good sign. He figured that if the men on this French ship were ignorant enough not to have heard of Moby Dick, then they might fall for his plan. He quickly paddled back to tell Ahab that this ship had no word of Moby Dick. Ahab then disappeared to his cabin, and Stubb returned to the *Rosebud*.

Holding his nose, Stubb climbed aboard the *Rosebud* and noticed that the first mate had torn rags stuffed up his nose.

"What's wrong with your nose? Did you have a nose bleed?"

"No. Just trying to plug it up," answered the unhappy man. "The smell got to me."

To be polite, Stubb said, "What smell? I don't smell anything. Fine day, isn't it?"

"What are you doing here? Is there something you want?"

"Yes," said Stubb, "could I speak with your captain?"

The first mate disappeared below the deck and returned with the captain of the *Rosebud*. He was a small man who looked too neat and tidy to be a sea captain. As it turned out, he was once a perfume manufacturer. Stubb realized that there could be no doubt that this

man was well aware of the ambergris and its value.

Still hoping his plan would work, Stubb lied, "Dear Captain, I feel I should let you know that just yesterday our ship met up with another ship whose crew had caught a deadly fever from a sick whale. The captain, first mate, and six sailors had died. If you don't want to risk your lives, sir, I'd suggest that you let that whale go immediately."

It worked! Instantly, the captain ran to his crew shouting to cut the chains and drop the whale. He then turned to thank Stubb, who was hurrying back into his boat.

Cleverly, Stubb guided the *Pequod* in between the *Rosebud* and the whale. The *Pequod* blocked the *Rosebud*'s view of the whale, and Stubb's boat was hidden as it fast approached the sick whale. Grabbing his sharp spade, Stubb began digging madly into the whale's side until the crew heard him shout, "I've got it, I've got it!"

Dropping his spade, he stuck both hands in and shoveled out handfuls of ambergris. He might have claimed more if it weren't for Ahab who was growing impatient and yelled that if Stubb didn't hurry up, they'd leave him behind.

Once things had settled down, it was discovered that during the dash for the ambergris, one of Stubb's oarsmen had sprained his hand. A replacement had to be found from the group of men who normally stayed on the ship while the boats chased the whales. One of these so called ship-keepers was a small black boy named Pippin, or Pip for short. Now Pip was a cheerful fellow, but rather timid and very softhearted. Why he was chosen to replace the injured oarsmen is one of those questions impossible to answer. Nevertheless, for whatever reason, Pip was now a part of Stubb's crew.

The first whale chase Pip went on, he was very jittery. When the killing was over, he was

greatly relieved to have escaped any contact with the whale.

Tashtego said to Stubb, "I detest that little weasel. You'd better tell him to bring along his courage next time."

During the second chase, when the whale was harpooned, Pip got scared and jumped out of the boat, paddle and all! Unfortunately, he landed right in the middle of some loose coils of line that happened to be floating on the water. When the whale took his usual flight and darted across the water, the line instantly tightened around Pip's chest and neck. Poor Pip! His face was turning blue and he was choking helplessly. The line had to be cut or he would die!

Tashtego was nearest to Pip, but he was so keen on the hunt, it looked as though he might just let Pip be squeezed to death! He couldn't bear the thought of losing this grand whale for the sake of saving miserable Pip.

"Cut! Cut!" screamed Stubb to Tashtego. Pip's eyes seemed to beg, "Yes, please do!

Please!" Finally, a half a minute after Pip went overboard, the line was cut.

Once he was recovered, Pip was heavily scolded by Stubb and Tashtego who told him that if he ever jumped from the boat again, they wouldn't pick him up. They said they were not about to lose any more whales because of him. Not learning his lesson, Pip jumped again when a second whale was harpooned. Luckily, this time he did not land in the line. But just as Stubb and Tashtego had threatened, Pip was left behind in the sea.

"He'll be okay," said Stubb who had no intention of truly abandoning the poor coward. "The boats behind will pick him up in a few minutes."

Unknown to Stubb, the other boats had spotted a pod of whales and were off for a chase in another direction. Pip was deserted! Hours later, just as he had surrendered his life to the sea, the ship by chance came upon him.

From that point on, Pip walked around the deck like a confused idiot. Although the sea had not taken his poor little body, his mind was drowned forever.

Let us not dwell on such tragedies and return to the whaling business. Many pages ago, when I explained the cutting in, I promised to tell you what happened to the blubber after it was sliced into Bible leaves.

At the front part of the deck, each whaling ship has what is called her try-works. The try-works are used to boil the oil out of the Bible leaves. They are like a huge stone oven with two enormous pots in them, called the try-pots. When not in use, the try-pots are polished until they sparkle enough to be used in a kitchen fit for a king! And sometimes, during the night, sailors will crawl into them and take a nap. It was about nine o'clock at night when the try-works on the *Pequod* were first lit and by midnight they were in full operation.

The men were kept busy either tossing blubber into the pots or keeping the fire going beneath. The blubber hissed, the flames roared, and the smoke billowed. The men worked until their eyes burned and their beards filled with greasy grime.

In the end, the oil lay cooling and then, while still warm, was transferred and sealed in enormous barrels. When the last pint was gone, the hatchway was opened and the barrels were taken down below.

This concludes my description, in all its detail, of the entire whaling process from the killing to the storing of the oil. And now I will reveal to you perhaps the most amazing part of the whole business.

On the day of the cutting in, the deck was covered with blood and oil, and the try-works were black with soot. Ropes, pulleys and hooks lay tangled and tossed in heaps; leftover whale's head was piled high, and tools were thrown everywhere. But a day or two after, as you

looked around, you would swear it was not the same ship. The decks had been scrubbed to their wood finish, the black try-works were silver again, all ropes were coiled neatly, and every tool had been washed and put away. There was not one clue on the *Pequod* that a whale had just been slaughtered.

It was not long after our clean up when we came upon an English ship named the *Samuel Enderby*. From across the water, one of their crew yelled, "Have you had any luck, men?"

We quickly reviewed our various catches, but before we could finish, Ahab yelled, "Have you seen the white whale?"

The captain, who had been resting in his boat's bow, stood up, saying, "You see this?" He held up his arm. It was white and made of sperm whale bone.

"Lower my boat!" ordered Ahab.

In no time, Ahab and his crew were in the water, and soon both captains were inspecting each other's limbs.

"Aye, aye, Captain! Looks like we're both partly made of ivory," said Ahab. "Now tell me, did the white whale take your arm off?"

"He was the cause of it, that's for sure."

"How did it happen? Tell me," said Ahab eagerly.

"Well, it was the first time in my life that I ever went hunting for the sperm whale. I'd never even heard of Moby Dick. One day we were after a pod of about four or five whales and my boat harpooned one of them. He took us on a wild ride going around and around in a big circle. All of a sudden, in the middle of the circle, up comes this great white whale. He had a wrinkled forehead and a deformed mouth."

"That's him! That's him!" shouted Ahab.

"He had harpoons sticking in near his right fin."

"They were mine! My harpoons!" roared Ahab. "Go on. Go on."

"Well, you'll never guess what happened!" chuckled the Englishman. "This whale swims

over to my line and starts snapping at it to try to cut it."

"Oh, yes, I've seen that before. It's the old story of the protective fatherly whale coming to free the young harpooned one. They're a caring bunch, they are. But what next? What happened to your arm?"

"I'm not sure exactly," continued the one-armed captain, "but when Moby Dick bit the line, it somehow got caught in his teeth. The weird thing was that we didn't know the line was caught and when we pulled on it, we ended up smack on Moby Dick's head! Well, I must say, he was the noblest and biggest whale I've ever seen! I decided right then to capture him, even though he was steaming mad. I jumped into my first mate's boat which was right next to mine, grabbed a harpoon, and sent it flying right into the whale's side. Before I knew it, the whale's white tail was straight up in the air like a grand old birch tree. I struggled to grab a second harpoon. Suddenly, as if the tree had been cut down, the tail fell on the boat, smashing it in two. My men and I were tossed right on top of the whale. I could see my first harpoon sticking out of his body. Suddenly, the whale took a dive. On his way down, the free end of the harpoon—you know, the end with the barb on it—caught me here, under the arm. It ripped my arm to shreds. It was a mighty bad wound."

"And did you see Moby Dick again after that?" asked Ahab.

"Twice."

"But you couldn't capture him?"

"I didn't even want to try. I've already given him a tasty first course, and I'm not about to give him my other arm for dessert. One arm's enough! No thank you, no more white whales for me. I do admit, though, it would be a great honor to kill the beast. And profitable, too! There's a ton of valuable oil in him. But I'm sure you'll agree, Captain, that he's not worth losing another leg over."

"How long since you saw him? Which way was he heading?"

"Good gosh," cried the Englishman, "you're not seriously thinking of hunting him, are you?"

"Tell me!" roared Ahab. "Which way was he heading?"

"To the East," answered the Englishman, and whispering in Fedallah's ear, he asked, "Is your captain insane?"

Fedallah put a finger to his lips to hush the man and then motioned for Ahab to follow him back to their boat. As the boat pushed off, Ahab stood with his back to the *Samuel Enderby*. The captain tried calling him to come back. Ahab, standing solid and still, ignored the cries. He was deep in thought as his boat came alongside the *Pequod*.

CHAPTER 13

A Crew in Misery

The *Pequod* was still heading toward Japan when it was discovered that several barrels of oil down below were leaking. Starbuck, being somewhat alarmed, went to report the problem to Ahab.

"Who's there?" growled Ahab upon hearing the footsteps at his door. "Go away!"

"Captain, it is Starbuck. And I've come to tell you that the oil is leaking, sir. We must anchor and send everyone below to find the leak."

"Now that we are nearing Japan? Are you crazy, man?"

"Well, sir, if we don't find that leak by the end of the day, we'll lose all the oil we've collected in the past year. And since we've come half across the world for it, don't you think it would be a good idea to try to save it?"

"Let it leak!" roared Ahab. "The only thing that'll be worth saving is a good story about Moby Dick's death!"

"But think of the owners back in Nantucket, sir. They won't be too pleased if all you return with is a story."

"The owners don't bother me, Starbuck, but right now you are. In fact, you are bothering me a lot. Get back on deck, now!"

Not moving, Starbuck said, "I think you should reconsider fixing the leak, sir."

"Back on deck, Starbuck, before I shoot you," ordered Ahab, reaching for a loaded musket.

"You've made me mad, sir, but I am not afraid of you. You have only to be afraid of yourself. Beware of yourself, Captain Ahab."

An hour later the captain appeared on deck and ordered that the ship be anchored just as Starbuck had suggested. Upon searching for the leak, barrel after barrel was hauled out onto the deck. Long-forgotten supplies that had been stashed away were piled on top of the barrels. It was so crowded that there was hardly any room to move. Eventually the leak was discovered and repaired and everything was taken back down below. Everything, that is, except the hundreds of rats and moles that had escaped from their hiding spots and were scurrying around the deck carrying deadly diseases. Poor Queequeg fell victim to one of these diseases.

Within a few days, Queequeg had wasted away so all that was left of him was bones and tattoos. As I sat by my friend's side, he held my hand so tightly that I knew he was begging me for help. I was filled with more sympathy than I ever thought would be possible.

One day, thinking he was going to die, Queequeg asked me an unusual favor. Where he came from it was a custom to preserve a dead warrior's body and then lay it in a canoe and send it out to sea. He knew that on a whale ship a dead man was wrapped in his hammock and thrown overboard for the sharks.

"Please," he asked me, "could the carpenter build me a canoe, or something out of wood, for my coffin?"

The carpenter was pleased to help Queequeg, and so, out of old planks, he skillfully constructed a wooden box. When the last nail was hammered in, he said, "Okay, Queequeg, you can die any time now."

Queequeg was anxious to see his custom-made coffin so the men brought it to him. He then asked for his harpoon and placed it in the coffin along with one of the oars from his boat. He added some biscuits, a container of water, and a pair of trousers which he rolled up for a pillow. Next, he had the men lift him in and close the lid. Queequeg lay there awhile, then called for the men to return him to his hammock.

"Okay, now I'm ready to die," he sighed.

It seemed that from the moment Queequeg was ready to die, he suddenly felt much better. Soon it appeared that there would be no need for the coffin after all. Queequeg simply said, "I've changed my mind. I think I'll stay around longer." The carpenter shrugged his shoulders and let out a big sigh.

This part of my story has told of the *Pequod*'s carpenter, and the next event will introduce you to our blacksmith named Perth. With a scruffy beard and wearing an apron, Perth was working at his oven when Ahab came along carrying a small bag.

"What are you working on there, Perth?" asked Ahab.

"I'm smoothing out this rusty old lance, sir."

"Isn't the metal too hard to smooth out?"

"No, I think I can do it, sir."

"Well, tell me then," said Ahab, "can you smooth out this forehead?" and he pointed to the scars just below his hair.

"That, sir? No, I can smooth out most things, but not that," said Perth.

"Ah, well, you're right blacksmith. I guess I have to live with a wrinkled forehead."

"A wrinkled forehead, sir?"

"Enough of such talk!" yelled Ahab, and then shaking his small bag, he said, "I want a harpoon made, Perth. The best harpoon ever. And here's what I want you to use." He emptied the bag onto a table. "These are nails from horseshoes."

"Horseshoes, sir? You won't find stronger stuff than that."

"I know. Now quick, Perth, make me a harpoon with a barb on the end of it sharper than a razor."

"Is this harpoon for the white whale, sir?"

"It's for the white enemy!" bellowed Ahab.

Perth smoothed and hammered the harpoon until it was ready for Ahab's final inspection. "A dent!" cried the captain. "Make it perfect, Perth."

Finally the harpoon satisfied Ahab and, armed with his new weapon, he retreated to his cabin.

A few weeks after Ahab's harpoon was made, the *Pequod* met a ship from Nantucket, the *Bachelor*. Having just filled her last barrels of oil, the *Bachelor* was heading home. There was no doubt that the men on the *Bachelor* were in good moods. On the deck, the mates and harpooners were dancing while fiddlers, with their glittering fiddles, played tunes from decorated mastheads.

We learned afterwards that the *Bachelor* had been very fortunate in its catches. Apparently, food had been dumped overboard so the barrels could be used to collect sperm oil. Every wooden item, except the ship itself, was chopped into kindling for the try-works. All

the kitchen pots and pans were filled with oil, even the kitchen sink.

It was quite a sight to see the two ships cross paths—one celebrated the good luck they'd had while the other worried about what was to come. This contrast was best illustrated by the two captains, standing on their decks.

"Come aboard! Come join in the fun!" cried the joyful captain of the *Bachelor*.

"Have you seen the white whale?" replied Ahab harshly.

"No, I've only heard of him. I don't believe in him, anyway. Come aboard!"

"You're too darned merry—no, thank you. You go your way, and I'll go mine," grumbled Ahab. And then, the *Pequod*'s captain turned to his crew and shouted, "They're heading home with a ship full of what *they* came for and we're still searching for what *we* came for, right men? Press on, men! Death to Moby Dick!"

"Aye, aye, Captain!" cheered the men, but with noticeably less enthusiasm than before. The crowd gazed longingly at the disappearing *Bachelor* wishing they could trade places with the jolly men.

Before sundown of that day, the *Pequod* met with the cruelest enemy on the Japanese seas—the typhoon. A typhoon is a severe hurricane that will sometimes burst out of a clear, blue sky without any warning.

Already the *Pequod*'s main sail had ripped and was waving in the wind like a torn handkerchief. When darkness came, the sky boomed with thunder and flashed with lightning. The waves looked like moving mountains. With every bolt of lightning, Starbuck glanced up at the masts worrying they'd be on fire. Stubb and Flask ordered the men to adjust the sails and tie the smaller boats tighter to the *Pequod*'s side.

"Look!" cried Starbuck, grabbing Stubb by the shoulder, "Do you see that the storm is

worse up ahead? That is the very direction that Ahab is heading for Moby Dick. We are doomed."

Disturbed by some noise, Stubb said, "Who's there?"

"Old Thunder!" answered Ahab.

Suddenly, the three masts caught fire like candles on a dining room table. The crew stood huddled together with their eyes fastened on the flickering lights. I couldn't help noticing that the three harpooners, each with his unusual appearance, looked more spooky than ever in the glowing flames. Daggoo seemed three times as tall, Tashtego's white teeth shone more brightly, and Queequeg's tattoos were as purple as an amethyst on a king's crown.

Ahab was caught in a spell. He cried, "Look up at the white flames men; they will guide us to the white whale!"

"No, old man, no—" begged Starbuck, "give up. This voyage is headed straight for bad luck. Let me turn the boat around and we'll head home."

The crew moaned together as if an agreement with Starbuck and ran to reverse the sails. At this instant, Ahab's harpoon, which was tied to the stern of the boat, caught fire. Ahab grabbed it and shook it in front of his crew as if to say, any man that so much as touches a sail will be poked with this burning torch. And then he spoke: "You promised to hunt the white whale and you are now committed to that promise as much as I am. Imagine that your fear is in this flame. I shall blow it out, and your fear will be gone!" Ahab leaned over the railings and extinguished the flame in the water. "There—now tell me, men, is your fear not gone? Are you not ready to continue our hunt?"

The crew's fear did not dissolve, but instead grew to almost a panic. With looks of terror, the men stared up at the three flaming masts which were slowly being extinguished by the pouring rain. It was midnight, and all they could do was pray that they would be alive to see the morning.

CHAPTER 14

More Bad Signs

D uring a violent storm when a ship is bounced around like a toy in a bath-tub, it is common for the ship's compass needle to spin uncontrollably. This was the case on the *Pequod* and we had no idea which direction we were going.

We were thankful when, some time after midnight, the storm eased up a little and the men were able to steer the ship back on course. The needle steadied itself. The crew sang joyfully as they took down the torn sails and hoisted up new ones. It appeared that the typhoon was over.

It was the first mate's job to report to the captain any changes that occurred on deck. Starbuck was on his way down to Ahab's cabin to tell him that the storm was over, when something caused him to stop just before knocking on the door. Lined up in a rack next to Ahab's door was a row of loaded muskets. Now Starbuck was an honorable man who had never hurt anyone before in his life. But seeing those guns and knowing what he could do with them was very tempting.

Slowly, ever so slowly, Starbuck picked up one of the muskets and inspected it. "Is it really loaded? Let me see—why, yes it is. I should put it down. Oh, but think what I could do. I could end this madness once and for all. We could all go home. Back to Nantucket to our families. Wouldn't that be wonderful! Why should Ahab be allowed to bring all thirty of us to our death? We have a right to demand that we turn around—we should cry mutiny! But didn't Ahab tell us all that if we rebelled he'd get us with his burning harpoon? We're trapped. Unless, of course, I free us all. One gun shot is all it would take. Look at me, I'm trembling all over. I can't do it. I just cannot do it. I'd better go in there and tell him what I came to say: That we're back on course and heading somewhere toward Moby Dick. Oh, how I hate that whale!"

He returned the musket to its place, wakened Ahab, and gave him the necessary information.

"Oh, Moby Dick!—" Ahab cried. "I'll find you at last!"

Next morning, the sea had calmed down significantly, but still rolled with long slow waves. The *Pequod* was pushed on in giant leaps. The sun shone brightly and everyone, except Ahab, was enjoying the change in the weather.

Ahab was staring at the sun with a puzzled look on his face. All of a sudden, he turned to the man steering the boat and yelled, "Which way are we heading?"

"Southeast, sir," said the steersman, for we were now supposed to be heading down across the Pacific Ocean toward the Equator.

"You're lying!" roared Ahab. "How can we be going east if the sun is at our back? It should be at our front, should it not?"

Every man on the ship was shocked. Ahab was right. In the morning the sun should have been rising behind us, but it was definitely rising in front. How could this be? The men watched as Ahab went to check the compass. For a moment he almost seemed to stagger. Sure enough, the compass was pointing east while the *Pequod* was, without a doubt, going west.

"The storm has turned our compass around—that's all," Ahab almost laughed. "Have you not ever heard of this before, Starbuck?"

"No, sir, that has never happened to me before," said Starbuck miserably. He was sure

that this was another bad sign. It was as if the ship had decided on her own that it was best to turn back.

It was ordered that the ship make a complete about turn. Realizing that his crew was a little uneasy about the upside-down needle, Ahab announced, "Don't worry, my dear friends. Out of this bit of steel, I can make a needle of my own that will point in the right direction."

Every man on the ship knew how difficult, and almost impossible, it was to rebuild an accurate compass. They waited nervously to see what the results would be. Finally Ahab called out, "Look men, our ship is going east and that's exactly what the compass says." Each man took his turn viewing the compass and, just as Ahab claimed, the instrument was in perfect working order. What a relief this was to the crew who did not want to be lost on the path across the world's largest body of water.

The morning after the compass mix-up was a calm sunny one. It was the first official day that the men at the mastheads were on lookout for Moby Dick. We were in the water where Ahab was sure he would find the white whale.

At sunrise on this particular morning, an unusual event occurred as the first sailor rose from his bunk to mount his masthead. Whether he was still half asleep or simply in a confused state, the man somehow tumbled from his spot. If he was sleepy before he fell, he was now wide awake, splashing frantically in the water.

Daggoo grabbed the life buoy, a small barrel that hung at the stern of the ship. He threw it out to the drowning victim, but cursed when he realized that it too was sinking. It had been damaged during the typhoon and nobody had thought to check it. Both man and buoy went down while the crew stood by helplessly.

No one on board the *Pequod* missed the meaning of this tragedy. The first man who went on lookout for Moby Dick was swallowed by the sea. Forgetting their sadness, the crew was filled with tremendous fear. To them this was another bad sign of the evil to come. Some even convinced themselves that the man was swallowed up, not by the water, but by Moby Dick!

As a result of this episode, the life buoy somehow had to be replaced. Starbuck could not find a barrel light enough for the job. Just as he was about to give up, he heard Queequeg's voice, "How about using my coffin?"

"A coffin for a life buoy?" exclaimed Starbuck.

"Yes, it does seem odd," said Stubb.

"It'll work though," concluded Flask.

So, the coffin was now a life buoy. The meaning of this, too, was not missed by the crew.

The next day a large Nantucket ship, the *Rachel*, was spotted heading for the *Pequod*. As the stranger neared us, one of our crew muttered, "She brings bad news. I can feel it in my bones."

"Have you seen Moby Dick?" cried Ahab.

"Yes, yesterday. But have you seen a whale boat? We've lost one of our boats."

Ahab was filled with excitement at the mention of Moby Dick, but he tried to hide his joy when he answered, "No, no lost boats around here."

Within minutes, the *Rachel*'s captain was on board the *Pequod*. Ahab pounced on him with questions about the white whale. "Where was he? Did you chase him? Tell me what happened."

Late on the afternoon of the previous day, three of the *Rachel*'s boats had been lowered for a chase. As they approached the group of whales, the white head of Moby Dick had suddenly risen out of the water. Instantly, the

Rachel's reserved boat was lowered to join in the chase for the great whale. From far away, the man at the masthead thought he saw the fourth boat being dragged by the white whale. As the boat grew smaller on the horizon, bubbling white water was seen on the water's surface. After that, there was nothing; the boat had completely disappeared.

Filled with worry, the *Rachel* picked up the three other boats before going in search of the fourth. And it was this mission that the *Rachel* was still on when it met us.

Having told his story, the *Rachel*'s captain now addressed the captain with the question he came on board to ask.

"Can the *Pequod* join forces with the *Rachel* in our hunt for the lost boat? Two ships working together could cover many more miles," said the distraught man to Ahab.

"No one searches that hard for a lost ship. Not during whaling season," Stubb whispered to Flask.

"I know," answered Flask. "I'll bet someone on that boat borrowed the captain's watch or something and he wants it back. That's got to be the reason."

"What a pathetic fool!" laughed Stubb.

"My son is on that boat," stated the captain.

"His boy!" gasped Stubb. "I take back all I said. Oh, how awful!"

"Please help me find my son," sobbed the man. "I'll pay you anything."

Ahab showed no emotion when he responded, "Captain, I will not do it. Already I have lost time. Starbuck, get rid of this man; in three minutes we shall move on."

"I can't believe it," said Stubb. Neither could Flask.

Looking hurt and rejected, the captain could do nothing but turn and head back to his own ship. Soon the two ships went their separate ways, but the *Pequod*'s crew watched in the distance as the *Rachel* sailed alone back and forth and back and forth across the water.

Three or four days slipped by after the meeting of the *Rachel* and Ahab was getting impatient. Every hour he yelled from his spot on the deck, "Men at the mastheads, what do you see? Any white water? Look hard for white water. Look hard!"

Finally, he could bear it no more and he announced, "I am going to watch for Moby Dick myself. I'm going to see him first. The gold coin shall be mine!" And he constructed a basket to sit in high in the air. He ordered Starbuck to hoist him up by a rope and then guard the tied rope on the deck. How funny that Ahab should ask Starbuck when Starbuck only recently was tempted to shoot him.

There Ahab sat, hour after hour, staring out for miles from his basket. It was an amusing sight and made even more amusing by a hawk that was flying overhead. All of a sudden, Ahab formed an umbrella over his head with both hands and yelled, "Is it raining? I didn't think it was supposed to rain." The crew dared not laugh out loud, knowing exactly where the "rain" had come from.

The *Pequod* continued on with its life-buoy coffin still swinging at the stern of the ship. Another Nantucket ship named the *Delight* was sighted. The name was not a good one, as we soon discovered. Hanging from her side were the remains of a smashed whale boat.

As usual, Ahab cried, "Have you seen the white whale?"

"Do you not see this wreck?" replied the sad-looking captain.

"Did you kill him?"

"No harpoon will ever do that!" said the depressed captain.

Perth, our blacksmith, took offense to that. He grabbed Ahab's harpoon and yelled, "You're wrong! This harpoon is so well made, it will be the one to kill the great monster."

"Then, I wish you well, men. Yesterday I lost four out of five men at sea. You sail over

their graves. Today I bury the fifth man, who came back from the hunt alive but died in the night." Then turning to his crew, he gave the signal and said, "Okay, lift the body—"

Unfortunately, the *Pequod*'s crew heard the corpse hit the water. And worse, sprinkles of water reached their skin from the deadly splash. No one dared make a comment.

As we steered the *Pequod* away, we heard one of the *Delight*'s crew laughing, "Look men, they're already prepared for what's to come! They've got a coffin hanging from their stern!"

The next day, against a clear blue sky, Ahab sat in his basket with his forehead more wrinkled than ever. He was deep in thought. Starbuck looked at the captain closely. Was that a tear that just dropped into the sea? Suddenly, Starbuck saw the old captain as a sad, hopeless man lost in a sea of unhappiness.

Ahab asked Starbuck to lower him to the deck. He turned to the first mate for comfort.

"Oh, Starbuck! It is a beautiful day, the same kind of day it was when I harpooned my first whale. And that was forty years ago. Imagine! Forty years killing whales! Forty years of loneliness on the dangerous sea! What a fool I've been. Why am I on this mission, Starbuck? Why? I'm so tired, so very tired. I feel weak and defeated. Starbuck, listen to me. When we go after Moby Dick, stay on the ship. I know you want to return home. Don't follow me. Let Ahab chase the white whale."

Starbuck was touched by his captain's sudden kindness and he was filled with hope. "Oh, Captain, no one should chase that monster. Let's turn around and go home. Let me go tell the crew. Oh, how happy we'd all be, Captain, to see old Nantucket again!"

Starbuck's words seemed to ring in Ahab's ears and, shaking all over, he shouted, "No. No. No. I've come for Moby Dick and I'll not leave until he's mine!"

Poor Starbuck! He was almost certain his captain would give up and head for home. Discouraged, Starbuck shuffled away with slouched shoulders.

CHAPTER 15

The Mission Ends

It was in the middle of the night when Ahab rose from his hammock and went to his special hole. Something in the air told him that a whale must be near.

At daybreak, Ahab roared, "Everyone on deck! Go to your duties! And you at the mastheads, look sharp! Look sharp for a whale!" He then instructed Starbuck to hoist him up in his bucket. Before even reaching the top, he cried, "Thar she blows! Thar she blows! It's Moby Dick!"

Aroused by the call, the men ran to the rails to catch a glimpse of the famous whale they had been chasing for so long. There he was, swimming grandly as if the whole ocean were his.

"Aha! The gold coin is mine!" shouted Ahab. "Look at that powerful spout! Look how he blows! Quick, lower three boats. Starbuck, remember, you stay on the ship."

Starbuck watched from the deck as the boats neared the enemy. Stubb was the first to speak, "Such a lonely looking beast."

"If I didn't know better," added Tashtego, "I'd say he almost looks gentle."

"Yes," agreed Flask, "there's a calmness about him, isn't there?"

Moby Dick swam on in this noble manner hiding his deformed mouth beneath the surface. Suddenly, he lifted his front part out of the water and there it was, that ugly mouth, in full view. It gave every one of us shivers. Then, with a good-bye wave of his flukes, he dove out of sight.

Ready for action at any moment, the men waited for Moby Dick's return. The water was dead still. It was an hour later when birds gathered together and fluttered wildly only a few yards from Ahab's boat. This was a sign that the whale was rising. Ahab looked down into the water and saw a white spot no bigger than a rabbit growing in size by the second. Ahab realized that Moby Dick was rising to the surface on his back with his jaws wide open. Suddenly, two rows of gleaming white teeth were thrust out of the water six inches from Ahab's head. Just then, one of the whale's teeth got caught in an oar-lock. With his jaws still wide open, the whale shook the caught boat causing the crew to tumble over each other and land in the boat's stern. Somehow Ahab was able to keep his spot at the bow. He reached to free the tooth when, at that instant, something slipped and both jaws snapped together like a pair of enormous scissors. The boat was completely cut in two. Ahab went flying into the water while the remaining crew floated away in the back half of the boat.

Moby Dick drew away and began swimming in a circle around the crew in the broken boat and Ahab, who could barely stay afloat. Fedallah tried desperately to pull Ahab on board the wreck, but the whale stirred the water so violently the two men couldn't grab hold of each other. The other three boats were unharmed and remained on the outer edge of the circle watching this spinning wheel that had Ahab as its center. They could see no way of breaking into the circle without causing Moby Dick to react.

Meanwhile, the crew observed all this from the ship's mastheads and the ship came sailing to the scene. Ahab shouted, "Sail toward the whale! Scare him off!"

The *Pequod* broke up the circle and as Moby Dick swam off, the boats raced to the rescue. The crew hauled Ahab's drenched and heavy body into Stubb's boat like an anchor.

"Where's my harpoon—" gasped Ahab. "Is it here?"

"Yes, sir, it was not thrown," said Stubb.

"And the men, are they all here too?"

"Yes, sir, all five of them," replied Stubb.

"Thank goodness. Now which direction did he go? Help me stand up so I can have a look. There, I see him over there. Tomorrow— we'll get him tomorrow."

By the time the three boats were tied to the ship, it was almost night. A voice from the masthead cried, "Can't see the whale anymore, sir; it's too dark."

"Where was he heading the last time you saw him?" asked Ahab.

"Straight in front, sir," responded the voice.

"Good. We'll keep on course and slow down a little; the whale will travel slower at night. Go now, men. Go get some sleep."

Knowing sleep would not come to him this night, Ahab went to his special hole and waited there until dawn. At daybreak, three fresh men took over at the mastheads.

"Do you see him?" asked Ahab.

"Not yet, sir."

You must wonder how, after the long night, Ahab could be so certain that he was still following the whale's path. By observing a whale before he goes out of sight, a good whaleman can make an accurate prediction of the direction that the whale will continue to swim, as well as the whale's speed.

We soon discovered that Ahab had accurately predicted the whale's direction, but had made a mistake on his speed. Moby Dick had travelled even slower than Ahab thought he would. And so, it was a great surprise when Moby Dick was spotted less than a mile from the ship.

This time the white whale was not calm. Oh no! He was breaching! Breaching is the marvellous act of rising at full speed from the deepest water and leaping high into the air. The wondrous splash can be seen seven miles away!

"Moby Dick!" cried Ahab. "Breach no more! Your time has come! Lower the boats, men— except for you, Starbuck."

By the time the boats were in the water, Moby Dick had turned and was coming for the three crews. You will remember that a whale cannot see anything directly in front of him unless it is far enough away. At this point, we were still at a distance where Moby Dick could see us. As the whale swam closer, every pair of eyes in the boats doubled in size, and then tripled, when Ahab announced that they would take the whale head on. He knew that within minutes they would no longer be in Moby Dick's vision. It was a clever idea, but it failed! As if knowing exactly what Ahab had planned, Moby Dick charged the boats while he could still see them. The men had no time to retreat.

The white whale rushed among the boats with snapping jaws and a flailing tail. By a miracle, the boats escaped his attack and three harpoons were successfully lodged. In a fury, the whale swam helter-skelter and ended up tangled in the lines. The more tangled he became, the closer he drew the boats to him as they were running out of line.

Ahab grabbed a knife and slashed his line. He freed himself, but Stubb and Flask were like flies caught in a spider's web. And when the whale made one last rush in the tangled lines, the two boats smashed into each other and blew to pieces. Everything spilled out into the churning sea.

As Ahab's boat rowed to the rescue, Moby Dick came up from below and slammed his forehead into Ahab's boat sending it flying through the air. Rolling over and over, the boat landed face down in the water and the men paddled frantically out from under it. The whale obviously decided that his job was done for the day and swam off at a steady pace with the lines dragging from his back.

Once again, the ship came and gathered all the floating men and pieces. When Ahab was helped to the deck, the crew gasped at what they saw. Ahab's ivory leg had broken off, leaving a sharp point like a splintered piece of wood.

"Let me lean on you, Stubb," said Ahab.

"Sure," Stubb replied as cheerfully as he could. "Too bad about your leg, sir, but at least there's no blood."

Ignoring Stubb, Ahab asked, "Which way did he go?"

"East, sir."

"Okay, men, follow him. And carpenter, repair those broken boats and make me a new leg. Hurry! Fedallah, we'll go out again. Fedallah?—where's Fedallah?"

"Haven't seen him, sir," said Stubb. "He didn't come in with the other men."

"Didn't come in? Not gone! He can't be gone!" cried Ahab.

"He must have gotten caught in your line, sir. I thought I saw him dragged under."

"My line? Not my line? Oh—it was all my fault! What kind of a monster am I? But where's my harpoon? Who's seen my harpoon? Oh yes, Fedallah threw it. It's in the whale, it's in the whale! I must get it back. After him, men— I'll murder him yet! Two days we've chased him. Tomorrow will be the third. Yes, men, we'll chase him once more, but you can be sure it will be the last time!"

With those words, Ahab gave the same instructions as the night before. The crew went to bed, but had trouble sleeping because of the hammering and sawing on deck. The carpenter and a group of helpers were busy repairing the day's damage.

By morning the spare boats were equipped with new tools and Ahab had a new leg. As soon as the sun creeped over the horizon, Ahab asked his usual question, "Do you see him?"

"Nothing, sir."

Noon arrived and there was still no sign of the whale. Ahab, growing impatient, said, "We've passed him. Must have. This is terrible! But how could it have happened? Oh, of

course, I should have thought of it. With all
those harpoons in him and the lines he's dragging he's much slower than normal. Turn
around, men, turn around. I will not have
Moby Dick chasing me!"

Starbuck grumbled to himself, "And now
we're sailing straight for his open jaws. I feel
as though I am already lying in my grave
chilled to the bone!"

A long hour passed and then Ahab finally
spotted the familiar spout. The crew sprang
into action and Ahab said to Starbuck, "Good-
bye. Keep a sharp eye while I'm gone. We'll
talk tonight while that whale lies tied to our
ship." Their hands met, and their eyes fastened. Starbuck almost begged the captain
not to go, but stopped himself knowing that it
would be useless.

Ahab gave the word and the boats were off.
They had not gone far when Ahab realized that
the whale had dove under. After some time, the
water suddenly rippled in big circles around

them. The whale was breaching again. There was a humming sound and with the men frozen in anticipation, the huge body shot out of the water draped with ropes, harpoons, and lances.

"Attack!" shouted Ahab.

With all the tools stuck in him to remind him of his anger, the whale once again charged the boats. The waves caused harpoons, oars, and lines to go flying out of Stubb's and Flask's boats.

As the whale got closer, the men let out a gasp. Caught in the lines wrapped around the whale's back was the ripped dead body of Fedallah. He was still clutching the harpoon. His ghostly eyes came right up in front of Ahab, and just then, the harpoon dropped from his hand. Ahab cried, "Oh, Fedallah, even in your death you are helping me! What a loyal man you are! I wish I could thank you."

Stubb whispered to Tashtego, "He'll be able to thank old Fedallah in person before this day's through."

Having gathered his thoughts, Ahab instructed the two other mates to return to the ship and collect spare equipment. During this slight pause, Moby Dick swam away and, in no time, had passed the ship. Ahab pulled his boat up to the *Pequod*'s side and, paddling along next to her, told the ship's crew to keep following the whale. Starbuck leaned over the railing and pleaded, "Oh, my poor captain! Quit—quit before it's too late! Look! Moby Dick is swimming away. He doesn't want to harm you. Don't you understand?" Ahab ignored the pleas.

The whale must have been tired from the three-day chase for he seemed to be slowing down. Before long, the ship and Ahab's smaller boat were right on Moby Dick's tail.

Ahab moved to the bow of his boat as it came alongside the whale. With fierce determination, Ahab lifted his arms high and then flung the harpoon deep into his enemy. In the next instant, the whale shot away so fast that the line snapped!

"Grab your oars, men! We can catch him. Speed ahead!" shouted Ahab.

Hearing Ahab's boat, Moby Dick spun around. As he turned, he first caught sight of the ship and, mistaking the ship for his attacker, he swam straight for her.

"Look! The whale's going to smash the ship!" screamed Ahab's frightened crew.

On deck, Starbuck, Stubb, and Flask saw the approaching whale and knew they were going to die. The *Pequod*'s crew stood motionless. There was nothing any of them could do. When the whale's forehead hit the ship's side, planks and men flew high into the air.

Under the falling pieces, Moby Dick turned in the direction of Ahab's boat. Ahab knew this was his last chance; he threw a harpoon for the second time that day. Once again, the whale took off. As the line uncoiled, it tangled and in a fatal move Ahab reached to clear it. The line caught him around the neck and dragged him overboard.

Moby Dick dove and the men, having completely lost their senses, didn't cut the line. Ahab's crew followed him down into the sea.

Not far away, the *Pequod* seemed caught in a whirlpool. All her men, every floating oar, and every lance and harpoon were spinning round and round. Eventually, every last bit of the *Pequod* was sucked in at the center of this whirling circle and never seen again.

I know that this is what happened to the *Pequod*. I know because I watched from the outer edge of that spinning circle clutching helplessly to a floating plank. And as each part of the *Pequod* vanished one by one, the seriousness of my situation became clearer to me. To be left to die a slow death on the water would be much worse than going under with the *Pequod*.

247

Miraculously, just as the water swallowed up the last speck of the *Pequod*, it coughed up something new in the distance. I squinted to see a ship rising out of the horizon. Was it possible? Would I be saved? I flailed my arms wildly on the water hoping to catch the ship's attention.

By the time the ship spotted me I knew it was the *Rachel* still searching for the captain's son. The captain would be disappointed to discover that it was only me, Ishmael, the sole survivor of the *Pequod*. *The sole survivor.* Why me? It was a question I would ask myself each night as I stood on the deck of the *Rachel* staring out into the surrounding water. For some reason, I had been chosen to live to tell a great tale of Moby Dick. A tale that ended with Ahab and all his hatred sinking to the ocean floor and Moby Dick swimming free. I knew that Moby Dick was the victor and, somehow, that made me smile.